FIFTEEN LOVE

A SELECTION OF SHORT AND TALL STORIES

With All Good Wishes

BY TOM TYLER

JACK OF ALL TRADES PUBLISHING

WRITTEN, PRINTED AND PUBLISHED IN ENGLAND

2010

Fifteen Love

This first edition published in 2010 by Jack of All Trades Publishing.

ISBN 978-09567463-0-6

PUBLISHED BY JACK OF ALL TRADES PUBLISHING, PRINTED IN ENGLAND BY THE LAVENHAM PRESS, ARBONS HOUSE, 47 WATER STREET, LAVENHAM, SUFFOLK. U.K. CO10 9RN.

Cover design and painting by Tom Tyler.

CONTENTS

DEDICATED TO MY WIFE, 'TRICIA

FORWARD AND ACKNOWLEDGEMENTS.

I have to admit to being a little hazy about these stories. I found most of them in a cupboard while looking for something else, - a not unusual occurrence round here. I guess that some were written as much as twenty five years ago, and then put away and forgotten. You may feel that was just as well!

The stories are a mixed bag. Seven of them were either based on stories told to me by my parents, or are elaborations of my own experiences. One is an expanded version of a story someone told me not so long ago. My very grateful thanks to the storyteller. Seven of the stories are pure works of fiction, as far as I know.

In "The Murdering Ring" there is an account of the death of Bishop James Hannington, first Bishop of Eastern Equatorial Africa, and for this account I acknowledge my debt to his biographer, E.C.Dawson.

Given that so many books of short stories have been written by famous authors, it seems most presumptuous of a very minor author to add to the pile, but when I dug these long forgotten stories out and re-read them, I did quite enjoy them, and my hope is that you may too, and that this small book may while away an hour or two on a tedious journey, or waiting at an Airport, as one does these days. It might even fit into somebody's stocking at Christmas time!

My very grateful thanks go to Lisa and the team at Lavenham Press for all their help in producing this book, and to my wife for being once again my invaluable proof reader.

Ipswich, October 2010.   Tom Tyler.

SHORT STORY ONE. THE COLONEL'S GNASHERS.

The Colonel sat by the fire, reading. Even when seated in his favourite wing chair, it was at once apparent that he was a tall man, and his greying hair and military moustache gave him a very distinguished appearance indeed. From beneath bushy eyebrows a pair of piercing blue eyes scanned the page of his book, and one almost expected him to sport a monocle instead of the light reading spectacles balanced on his long, straight nose. Even when dressed informally, as now, in a smoking jacket and corduroy trousers, he always wore a tie, inclining towards one of his now faded regimental old favourites. He was what one would have described as a "fine figure of a man" even with the spectacles, about which he was a little self conscious.

The other thing that he was even more self conscious about was a deeply kept secret. People sometimes noticed that the colonel rarely laughed out loud, usually managing at best a tight lipped smile or a sort of chortle. They put it down to his military training, strict upbringing, or something like that. In fact, the true reason was that the colonel had false teeth. Many years of poor dental supervision in India in the 1930s had taken their toll, and by the end of the war the colonel's teeth had totally ceased to be his original issue. However, the colonel was very secretive indeed about this fact, and apart from his wife and his dentist, to his knowledge no-one else was aware of the problem and its solution.

A slight frown appeared across his face. The book he was reading had been recommended to him by a very persuasive friend, and frankly it was not the sort of book the colonel usually read. It was rather too modern, too explicit. He had just navigated into a rather naughty passage involving the heroine, an implausibly attractive young lady, and a roguishly nautical gentleman. The outcome of this meeting on the high seas was not hard to predict, and the colonel felt a little flushed and embarrassed. He looked up, peering over the top of his spectacles. His wife sat in her accustomed chair on the opposite side of the hearth, also reading, but knitting simultaneously by using the special book rest he had designed and made for her in his workshop. She was now absorbed in what she was reading, and she did not notice his slightly furtive glance.

The colonel found the place in his own book once again, but his concentration had been interrupted, and even the ever closer proximity of the two shipmates failed to hold his attention. Should he be reading such a book, he asked himself? But then he had once had his own naughty moment, hadn't he?

His mind skipped back over the years. He had indeed been the model of an army officer, efficient, dedicated, wedded to his great regiment, - and a bachelor, of course. Always ready to be sent on duty wherever the army needed him to be, without the encumbrance of a wife and family. After the war, which brought him well deserved distinction and promotion, he had settled down to a semi-retired life, though still only in his early fifties. He spent his time partly based in his club in London, so convenient for many activities and meeting up with old friends, and partly down at his little cottage in Wiltshire, situated close to the firing ranges on Salisbury plain. The colonel could always distinguish which type of gun was being fired, for the benefit of any visitors.

In between these two bases the colonel would "go off on exercises" as he liked to term it, gently touring round southern England in his stately pre-war Rover saloon, and visiting old friends whom he had known since he first joined the army. He was truly a man of routine and order, and every autumn found him in South Devon, visiting two old friends who lived in the neighbourhood of Torquay. Devon in October could be a lovely county to explore, and Torquay could be surprisingly warm and devoid of summer visitors.

The colonel's plans always followed the same pattern year by year. He would drive gently down from Wiltshire, taking about four hours for the journey, with a stop near Honiton. He would then arrive at the Avalon Hotel in Torquay, park his car, take possession of his usual room, have his luggage brought up, and it would be exactly time for afternoon tea. The hotel was situated on the top of a low hill about half a mile from the sea, and the colonel could look out across Torbay from his bedroom window, and satisfy himself that everything was in order.

It was an old fashioned hotel, largely untouched since it had first been built in the 1920s, and it suited the colonel excellently. It was comfortable, solid, and with no modern frills or fads about it. The staff, all of mature years and very quiet and experienced, matched the hotel perfectly. It might not boast separate bathrooms for every room, and all that nonsense, but the colonel could happily make do without such things. His army training had taught him to rough it in many and varied situations, - in India you had been lucky to get an old bucket half full of dirty water on many an occasion. The chairs and beds at the Avalon were very comfortable, and the food was excellent, again without any of the modern messing around. The colonel indulged himself in a short mouth-watering daydream!

After his tea, and a chat to one or two members of staff, whom he regarded as old friends, the colonel went upstairs to unpack his cases and get his room tidy, as for inspection. Then it was time for a leisurely bath before he dressed for dinner. On this first night he always went out to the select restaurant on the quay by the Inner Harbour, where he met his friends and their wives, and over dinner they caught up with all the news of the past year. They would then plan some expeditions together for the fortnight of the colonels' stay in Torquay.

Fifteen Love

That particular year all went according to plan at first. The crumpets for tea, together with scones, clotted cream and home made strawberry jam, all made the journey down to Devon entirely worth while. His usual room was as welcoming as ever, with the sea just visible under a rising moon as darkness set in. The colonel hummed a favourite tune from "H.M.S. Pinafore" as he walked along the short corridor to the bathroom. There were very few other guests staying in the hotel at that season of the year, so he felt he had almost exclusive use of it anyway. The bathroom was just as he would have expected to find it, and in a few minutes he was wallowing contentedly in the old-fashioned bath full of gloriously warm water.

He had not been occupying the bath for more than a few minutes when an unusual and disturbing event occurred. Someone came along the corridor, paused, and then rattled the brass doorknob on the bathroom door. This, the colonel knew, was not only bad manners, but also quite unnecessary. The original maker of this door had carefully fitted a sliding brass bolt on the inside of the door, which cunningly connected to a brass dial on the outside, above the doorknob. When the bathroom was in use, and the bolt pushed across to lock the door, the little dial on the outside proclaimed "Engaged." When the door was unlocked, and the bathroom empty, the dial would reassure the next hopeful visitor that it was "Vacant." It was foolproof and quite clear, even for the simple minded and unobservant!

The footsteps went away, and the colonel resumed his warm and comforting wallowing. But within five minutes it happened again!

The colonel could hardly believe it, and had to restrain himself from barking out a loud and peremptory command. He began to hurry over his bath, and much resented having to do so. It quite spoilt his whole evening. A few minutes later, just as he was balanced precariously on the edge of the bath, with one foot out, and the other being dried, it happened again. The colonel nearly fell forwards into the emptying bath, he was so staggered. He felt both angry and agitated. Somehow, he now felt guilty for just being in the bathroom at all. Considerably dishevelled, he grabbed his towel and sponge bag, and crept to the door. There was now silence outside. Quietly and slowly he slid back the bolt, opened the door, and peered out. The corridor was mercifully empty. With surprising speed and stealth for a man of his size, the colonel slipped along the corridor, almost keeping his head down to avoid enemy observation, and gained the blessed sanctuary of his bedroom. Entering, he was in the act of closing the door very softly, when two things happened. First, the colonel realised with dismay that he had not got his false teeth with him. Second, he heard the distinctive sound of the bathroom door being firmly shut and bolted.

The colonel sat down on the chair by his table, and reviewed the situation like a good military commander. His teeth were on the ledge of the washbasin in the bathroom. He had cleaned them and carefully placed them there before having his bath. He had forgotten to pick them up when beating a hasty retreat from the bathroom. There was now no way of retrieving them if the bathroom was occupied, and the door shut and locked. On the other hand there was no way he could go out to a smart restaurant for dinner with his friends without his teeth, - the prospect was so appalling that he ruled it out at once.

Yet there was still about an hour until he was due at the restaurant, though he would have liked to have been there by 7.25.p.m. to maintain his reputation for impeccable punctuality. Being late was just a form of rudeness, he had always taught his junior officers. The colonel spent a few minutes tidying his room, then crept quietly along the corridor to the bathroom. The door was indeed shut, and declared itself totally

"Engaged." From within, the colonel could hear the noise of water sloshing about. Even in his desperate predicament, being a perfect gentleman, he did not stoop to touching the door handle, but returned quietly to his bedroom. Three quarters of an hour still remained.

At five to seven the colonel crept along again. Now, to his amazement and dismay, he could clearly hear a voice from within the engaged bathroom uplifted in song. A female voice. And there was still the sound of water sloshing about. The colonel returned to his bedroom in a state of increasing desperation.

By 7.15.p.m. the colonel was frantic. He stood outside the locked bathroom door and listened to the continuing and somewhat louder singing from within. If he hadn't been so preoccupied with his own problem he might have even recognised that the singing water nymph had a very pleasant voice. As it was, the singing only made him feel all the more desperate.

Then his eye alighted on the little brass dial fixed to the door once again. Memories of childhood came back to him. Of visits to an uncle and aunt who had a lavatory on the upper floor, with just such a lock on the door. He had discovered after some experiment that you could manipulate the little dial with a finger, and slide the locking bolt back from the outside. He had several times done it successfully to the great annoyance of his female cousin, until his exploits had been detected by a prowling aunt, with exceedingly painful results. The colonel's finger strayed almost unconsciously to the little dial, and began to exert a gentle sideways pressure. The dial moved. Inside the bathroom the singing continued, even louder if anything. The colonel took a deep breath. He was a man of action, and this was a time for decision followed by action.

Slowly and carefully he slid the dial round with his forefinger, until it proclaimed "Vacant." He knew now, from past experience, that the bolt had slid back from its staple inside the door. The singing continued unabated from within. The colonel took another deep breath, and with infinite care turned the door handle, and then began to open the door. There was no break in the song, which he noted was a version of "Annie Laurie." He knew that the occupant of the bath should be facing the taps, with her back to the slowly opening door. The door opened against the bath, and the wash basin, hopefully still holding its treasure, was beyond. The colonel took a stealthy step into the bathroom, then another. There, shining like pearls in the lamplight, were his precious teeth exactly where he had left them. The colonel averted his face from the bath, partly out of gentlemanly propriety, party out of a desire to avoid future recognition, and took another step towards his goal, and then two more.

The scream, when it came, was no less of a shock for all that it was quite expected. The colonel felt as though he had jumped six feet into the air. For a moment he froze, irresolute, - something he had never done before, even in the heat of battle. Then he plunged forward towards the wash basin, dimly aware of strange noises from the direction of the bath. He almost cried out in triumph as he seized his teeth, and turned to escape by the way he had come. But in doing so, the colonel turned instinctively to his right, as in a military about turn, and his eye was arrested by the sight of a pink mountain in the centre of the bath, - no head, no feet, just a large pink island in the middle. Then, as the colonel watched, hypnotised, the water nymph ran out of breath and surfaced. He saw her gulp in a large breath, ready to scream again.

Even as he remembered this moment of crisis, the colonel could never account for his actions in the bathroom so long ago. In some pantomime he had first seen it done, probably by Widow Twankey or the like, and he had never forgotten it. In fact, when on his own, and quite private, he had practised doing it from time to time. You could hold a set of false teeth in one hand, just so, and by moving thumb and fingers make them gnash together very realistically. He had taken a childish delight in perfecting the trick for himself.

Now, faced with a very unpromising audience, and for the first time in his life, he gave one of his best performances. Advancing towards the bath quickly he transferred the teeth to his right hand, and as the lady in the bath opened her mouth to scream again he gnashed the teeth within a couple of inches of her shapely nose, and then as she rolled and submerged he made a plunging gnashing gesture towards each of her shapely buttocks. Then he fled back through the door, leaving it slightly ajar in his haste. There was a merciful silence from the bathroom.

For the first time ever the colonel was late for dinner. It was obvious that his friends were surprised, and that they detected that he was out of breath, and somewhat discombobulated. He offered no excuse, and was somewhat preoccupied during the meal. After parting from his friends, he took a turn along the sea front, partly to give himself time to collect his thoughts and assess his tactical position, and partly to avoid returning to the hotel until all the other guests had gone to bed. This latter he achieved very satisfactorily.

He spent a largely sleepless night, something that had not happened to him since the war ended. In the early hours of the morning he decided that his strategy should be to get up early and be first in to breakfast, - women never got up early in the morning. Then he would slip out of the hotel and go up on Dartmoor, if it was a fine day. Get some fresh air into his lungs, and think out his next move. In the event he was up long before he needed to be, and was actually waiting outside the dining room door when a rather surprised waiter opened it.

"Sorry to be in a hurry" he said," I wanted to make an early start now that the days are drawing in, and we don't get so much of an evening."

The colonel foreshortened his usual breakfast menu, with great regret, and ate hurriedly, hardly daring to have a second cup of coffee. The staff service seemed to him to be incredibly slow, as there were only three of them having breakfast at that moment. From his position at his table, he commanded a clear view of the door, and as the long minutes passed he became more and more nervous.

He was about to fold up his napkin, preparatory to rising and leaving, when the door opened. Even before he could see the person coming in he knew in his heart who it would be, and he was not disappointed.

A little smile crept across his face as he remembered so vividly, even after all these years. She had stood there, one hand on the door handle, just beautiful in every way. She had looked at him, eyebrows a little raised, and then she had smiled, a smile that at once demonstrated both friendship and humour, with a hint of something secret and exciting thrown in.

Almost unconsciously the colonel looked across at his wife, sitting opposite him. Something made her look up at exactly the same moment, and he was thrilled again to see exactly the same smile light up her face.

TWO. THE STONE WHICH THE BUILDER ACCEPTED.

The local people in the village call it Holloway Hill, but as a family we always called it Vicarage Hill for it linked the Vicarage, a lovely old Georgian house on the southern edge of the village, with the main village street. If the vicar decided to walk to his church, half a mile away, he first had to descend Vicarage Hill, which was about one in five steep, and with high banks each side, as much as fifteen feet high in places. On the hill two cars could just manage to squeeze past one another, taking great care, for many a piece of shiny black paintwork suffered severe grazing as a reward for the careless and speedy. It was an unwritten rule that cars coming up the hill had right of way, - a rule of the road probably dating back to the days in the West Country when cars climbing the steep hills, if stopped, had great difficulty in getting started again. I remember hair raising reversing back to the bottom of a hill so that one could have a second try! One fervently hoped you would not meet another adventurer trying to get a good run at the hill in his turn. When it snowed, or froze following rain, the whole game became even more fun!

At the bottom of Vicarage Hill, on the east side, are a couple of semi-detached cottages, built with the local grey granite stone, and roofed with local slates from the slate quarry in the next village, now long disused. Penn Quarry, with its mounds of broken slates, has become a favourite place for Adders to sun themselves on hot summer's days. Most of the village houses are built this way, but it's not so easy to get the granite now, so most of the "town" houses and bungalows built since the Second World War are constructed of brick, with tile roofs.

The cottage nearest to Vicarage Hill was bought in the 1960s by a Mr. Spendlove, a retired Civil Servant from up London way, who in fact had previously lived in Harrow. He moved

16

into his new home in the late spring, and he and his wife set about tidying up the somewhat neglected cottage. First, they decided to re-name it. The old name, Hill Cottage, had been in use for several centuries, but it did not appeal to them as it was "too ordinary" so they re-named the cottage "Hay Tor Cottage" after one of their favourite spots on Dartmoor. This puzzled the locals a good deal, as there was no way you could see Hay Tor or even a bit of Dartmoor from any of the bedroom windows of the cottage, due to it's location in the valley between the two hills.

After a few years of ruthlessly tidying up the unruly garden, and to re-decorating the exterior, - the woodwork was all repainted pink, a colour the Spendloves fondly believed to be most appropriate in a rural Devon village, the couple turned their attention to the inside of their cottage, and resolved on some fairly drastic alterations. The two small and cosy reception rooms should be knocked into one worthy room, the chimney could then be re-sited on the outside wall, and a pleasant porch added.

Mr. Spendlove had just cashed in a long standing insurance policy with very satisfactory results, and he and his wife resolved to do the work in style. A local architect of repute was appointed to draw up the necessary plans, get planning permission and supervise the work. It was also Mr. Spendloves resolve that only granite stone should be used for the work, so that it would harmonise with the rest of the cottage stonework. Woodwork would be painted a matching pink. The new fireplace on the external wall would also be built of granite, with an oak mantelpiece. The Spendloves talked of nothing else but their proposed renovation work for weeks, and their friends and neighbours got heartily sick of the topic.

Although Mr. Spendlove had hoped to keep the total cost of the work under the £2000 mark, the contract was put out to tender among local builders within a 20 mile radius, and when the tenders were eventually received it was found that a local builder, Mr. Hannaford, had submitted the lowest estimate. Mr. Charles Hannaford was a builder of the old school, a small and rather round man of uncertain years, who was never parted from his old battered hat winter or summer. He wore faded blue overalls, and drove a battered Rover family saloon car which dated from the later 1930s. His wrinkled and weather beaten face sported a prominent and rosy nose which glowed in direct proportion to the owner's recent consumption of scrumpy cider. Charlie was inclined to do most of his building measurements "by eye" and it must be admitted that over many years he had become very skilled at estimating measurements in this manner. New-fangled instruments like levels and even spirit levels were largely beyond him, and he was seldom seen even using a carpenters rule. But he could estimate the lie of the land, or the fall of a drain with almost unerring accuracy. It must be said that he was also a very obstinate man, who hated having to admit that he was wrong about anything.

Charlie employed two casual assistants, which is the best way of describing the total workforce of his building firm. Bert Easterbrook was his bricklayer and general odd job man. Bert spent a lot of his time mixing concrete or cement, and muttering under his breath. Harry Palfrey, the other half of the work force, was called in to drive the ancient lorry and to fetch building materials when required. When not required for work he skilfully poached salmon in the nearby river Dart, and pheasants wherever he could find them, and it was surprising how often he was successful. The lorry, which also has an important place in our story, was an old Bedford five tonner, built like a tank, and though it was a little younger than Charlie's Rover, it could well have seen service in the war before Charlie bought it as "an absolute bargain." It has to be admitted that Harry was actually very clever at keeping it on the road, and in those days before the dreaded MOT Test it climbed the steep Devon hills with a remarkable agility. Going down the hills was even more exciting, for Harry was not nearly so good at brakes as he was with engines. However, Harry had fitted it with a superb horn, which he had "borrowed" off a Bentley in a garage he had visited, while the owner was looking in the other direction, and the old lorry could be heard for miles on a clear day.

On a still, clear December day Charlie and his team arrived at Hay Tor Cottage to start work on the great project. It was a cold day, but that was nothing to the frigid reception they received from the Spendloves, for they had been supposed to start work the previous June. Charlie had indeed declared to the Spendloves

"I can tell ye you'll 'ave a bootiful fire a burning in that there new fireplace come next September, mi dears."

His excuses for the many ensuing delays would make a short story on their own, and a pretty comical one at that! Now the unfortunate Spendloves had to face the prospect of the extensive work being done during the depths of winter, with icy blasts hurtling through the cottage, and a totally disrupted Christmas and New Year. As a result, however, they had decided to be thoroughly extravagant, and spend some more of the insurance money on the luxury of Christmas at a Hotel in Torquay, and they justified this by saying that with all they had put up with they deserved a bit of pampering. Now they were so fed up with all the frustrations and delays, they just wanted the work done as quickly as possible.

The building work had not progressed very far when more difficulties became apparent. Charlie and his workforce might show great enthusiasm and ability when it came to demolition work, both knocking holes in walls and indeed knocking whole walls down with gay abandon, and covering the whole region in a thick layer of granite dust as they did so. But when it came to reconstruction, it was not nearly so easy or so speedy, and especially because Charlie did not seem to have his supply of necessary building materials at all well organised. The lorry arrived one day with a few slates, - a couple of dozen at most, which Charlie just happened to have tucked down behind his garage at home against the day when they might be useful.

"Ah always seys somefink like them slates will come in useful one day, and blow me look at em now, just the ticket for t'job," he declared to a very unimpressed Mr Spendlove.

Wood, in all sorts of shapes and sizes was fetched by Harry from a number of scattered sources, and dumped on the front lawn.

"It quite looks as though you are establishing a regular timber yard in the front garden" remarked Mr Spendlove, with more than a hint of sarcasm.

"'Tis just what us needs, mi dear" replied a happy Charlie, thinking he was being praised for his efforts for once, "Now us can allus find just what us wants without 'aving to go out for it."

Mr Spendlove gave up the unequal battle!

But finding the necessary granite remained a problem. At length Charlie was in the pub one evening as usual, and heard a whisper of some granite going begging in a builders yard over the back of Ashburton, and the following morning Harry was bidden to get over there at top speed and lay hands on it before someone else got to it first.

There was not a lot of the stone, but beggars couldn't be choosers, and with the help of a chap in the yard Harry got it loaded onto the old lorry. It was past lunchtime by the time he set off on his return journey, and he had not gone very far when he experienced a not unusual mishap in the old lorry. The steering began to feel heavier and heavier, and when he stopped by the wall of Landscove Churchyard, and climbed down from his cab, a quick inspection confirmed his worst fears. His right front tyre was already resting on the rim of the wheel.

Charlie went and unstrapped the spare wheel from under the tailboard, and rooted out the ancient jack. At least he knew exactly where that was, having had to use it only a couple of weeks before. He wondered as he surveyed the scene whether the jack would be strong enough to hold the lorry with its load of granite. It was lucky, reflected Harry, that it was the front wheel that was flat.

After a much needed cigarette, Harry set to work. This wheel had not been off for sometime, judging by the locked wheel nuts, and it took all his strength to get them loosened. He had another cigarette.

About half an hour later, after much puffing, swearing and groaning, Harry had substituted a spare wheel if anything more decrepit than the one he had taken off. He leaned against the Churchyard wall, trying to get his strength back with the help of another very limp cigarette. The afternoon was now well advanced, and out of the corner of his eye Harry noticed a rabbit moving between the gravestones in the growing dusk. He kept as still as a statue, and the rabbit hopped a bit nearer to him, and then disappeared behind a large stone that was propped against the wall. Harry quietly scaled the low wall, stealthy as a cat, and crept up on his quarry. He just succeeded in touching the rear end of the rabbit, but it was much too quick for him, and moreover it had an emergency exit all lined up ready. Harry swore loudly as it scuttered away across the churchyard, weaving its way between the graves with consummate skill. Slowly Harry eased the lump of granite away from the wall, in the vague hope that there might be another rabbit hidden behind it. He was disappointed. But though he was rabbit less, Harry was surprised to find that the slab of granite was not as heavy as he had expected it to be. Harry stood, holding it vertical, and pondered. Was it worth the effort to try to add it to the load of granite already on his lorry? Would Charlie be pleased with him, and commend him for his initiative? There didn't actually seem to be much in it for him, but it would befuddle the pesky rabbit the next time it tried to hide there. Next time he happened that road he would bring his gun with him. He squinted in imagination along the barrel at a fat rabbit! This last thought decided Harry, and he bent down and heaved the stone sideways onto the top of the low wall. With some further difficulty, and some very colourful language, he slid the stone across onto the top of the load on the lorry, which groaned in agony as it received the extra weight.

Harry brushed off his hands on his overall trousers, and climbed up into the cab. The rest of the journey, just three miles, was accomplished without incident, and it was getting dark when Harry and his gently steaming lorry arrived at the cottage to off load. Charlie was not pleased at the long time the expedition had taken, but fortunately both he and Bert were there to help with the unloading of the heavy load. When Charlie grumbled at the quality of the granite, and expressed the view that it was hardly worth the collecting of it, Harry pointed out the large stone from the graveyard.

"Look at that 'un then, maister," he said. "That un'll be a praper treat for to go above the fireplace wot we're a building of."

Charlie examined the stone in the rapidly fading light, and spotted the writing carved into the main face of the stone.

"'Tis got some writing on it yere" he muttered. "Where did ye get it tue then?"

Harry was immediately on the defensive, and for a time wondered whether to concoct some story about how it fell onto the back of his lorry just where he had happened to park it.

"Dudent matter nohow about that there writing," he argued, "yu can put that there side of it alongside of the wall, and no-one will see it at all that-aways."

Charlie said with a hint of reverence in his voice "This 'ere stone looks to me like a tomb stone, so it does, at least a bit of a one, anyways."

Harry looked even more guilty, and turned away to unload more of the granite from the back of the lorry. He did not wish to prolong the discussion. It was dark by the time they had got the last of the load off and stowed away, and once the stone had been stacked up they tidied up a bit, for it was the day before Christmas Eve, and it would be three days before they returned to the job, and only then if the weather permitted.

The day after Boxing Day dawned cold, dry and bright, -too bright for those who like Harry and Bert had enjoyed a very merry Christmas, and now found shining lights caused immediate headache! Charlie was the first on the scene of their labours. To begin with, as he wandered round in something of a daze, everything seemed exactly as they had left it. Then he glanced over at the pile of granite stones, and something about it made him give it a second glance. He had not really seen it in daylight before, and now he went over to take a closer look at it. Somehow it gave the impression that some bloomin kids had been messing around with it. On top of the pile was the large stone with the writing on it, but hadn't that stone been at the bottom when they had unloaded the lorry?

"How've that happen then?" asked Charlie out loud. He took off his battered old cap and scratched his head. "That un came off lorry furst, so 'e went to the bottom, surely?"

Beneath the large stone were two small pieces of granite which were now fractured, and no good for anything. Charlie swore. He heaved the large stone up, slid it off the pile, and propped it against the nearby fence, with the writing hidden from sight. For some reason he couldn't explain he didn't want the Spendloves or anyone else to see it. It gave him an uncomfortable feeling somehow, and he quietly cursed Harry for having picked it up and brought it along.

In due course the other members of his team arrived, and work began very slowly, at a suitably post-Christmas tempo. The outside wall was patched with the granite, and then they would be ready to start on the new fireplace the next day. Everyone agreed it would be a splendid idea to knock off a bit early, and be fresh in the morning.

Charlie was again the first on the scene the next day. It had been a calm winter's night, with quite a heavy frost. Charlie heaved himself out of his car, and then stood looking around with a look of total disbelief. To his great surprise the wooden fence had been flattened almost along its entire length, and lying on top of it, almost triumphantly, was the large slab of granite. Charlie was quite sure that the weight of the granite stone alone could not have brought the whole fence down like that, and why was the stone now lying with the writing clearly visible in the morning sun, when Charlie was quite sure he had propped it against the fence with the writing at the back, hidden from view? With much heaving and grunting the builder rolled it back and laid it face down on top of the now diminished heap of granite stones.

Charlie then set to work to try and resurrect the wooden fence before Mr Spendlove saw its sorry state. With the aid of Bert, who fortunately arrived more or less on time, he got it all propped up again, and put some spare stakes in to support both the upright posts, which had been snapped off at ground level.

" 'Twas some power that snapped off they old posts, maister" remarked Bert.

Charlie was thinking just the same thing, but he didn't say anything, but grunted in assent. He still couldn't remember there being any wind in the night. Could it have been a group of those young varmints coming this way after the pub had closed for the night? And why was the slab turned over to show its writing? All ways it seemed a real bit of a mystery.

Bert and Charlie set to work on the fireplace that was to be Mr. Spendloves pride and joy, and in due course a rather bedraggled Harry joined them, displaying evidence of an evening spent in the pub again.

"Did 'e see anyone cum up this way when pub closed?" Charlie asked him, trying to sound only faintly interested.

Harry took off his battered cap and scratched his head.

"Don't think so, boss" he replied. Actually he had not noticed a great deal when he stumbled out of the door of the pub at 11.p.m.

Charlie grunted, and resumed the slow process of building the new fireplace, which was rather like assembling a huge jigsaw puzzle. The large granite stone fitted in over the lintel, with its writing completely hidden, to Charlie's relief. The new wooden mantelpiece rested on top of it, and towards the end of the afternoon they fitted it in place, and the job was finished.

"'Tis a real ole praper job" remarked Charlie with satisfaction. The other two agreed with him that it looked just wonderful. It was quite late when they knocked off, having spent some time admiring their handiwork, but they felt justified in calling in at the Church House Inn on the way home, for a minor celebration.

Charlie was unusually cheerful when he got up in the morning, humming snatches of his favourite songs. He was still feeling the warm glow of pleasure because of the splendid fireplace he had created, and he felt Mr Spendlove would be very impressed when he saw it. He looked forward to admiring it again when he returned to the cottage after what promised to be a very good breakfast. But when Charlie let himself into the cottage, took off his cap and hurried through into the living room, he stopped deal almost in shock. He passed his hand across his eyes, in disbelief, hardly able to take in what he was seeing.

His new splendid fireplace had all but collapsed. The main lintel had cracked and given way, and several of the other stones on each side had fractured as well. It appeared the whole construction might fall forward into the room at any moment. Charlie was appalled. For a time he could only stand and stare at it, rooted to the spot. There was no logic in it that the builder could detect, and he was utterly bewildered as to the cause of it. Bert joined him in a few minutes, but though they had a lively discussion, he could throw no further light on the reason for the collapse. Together they began to very carefully dismantle the wreckage, taking care not to do any further damage. In the fullness of time Harry joined them, and was at once sent off with the lorry to scour the countryside for some more granite to replace the now broken and useless stones.

"But donne bring me any more o they ole slabs with writing on 'em" ordered Charlie, with more than a hint of anxiety in his voice.

In fact the large stone with the writing on it seemed to be the only one intact and undamaged among them all. Charlie regarded it with a look of considerable malevolence. He and Bert spent the morning trying to do a credible rebuilding work, and Harry rejoined them about lunchtime with the lorry and a small load of granite stones, which were all he had been able to locate. The whole task seemed twice as hard as before, and Charlie found he could summon up little enthusiasm for it, compared to the previous day.

"Twas bad enough doin it the once" he muttered, and Bert agreed with him.

Thank goodness it was a Friday, and the New Year was coming up as well. They knocked off a bit early, leaving the fireplace far from finished. The stone with the writing on it was left lying on the floor, together with some other bits of granite and the wooden mantelpiece. Charlie wouldn't have cared a jot if he never set eyes on it again. He travelled wearily home, having bidden his team a "Happy New Year." They would not meet again until Tuesday, and that was also the day that the Spendloves were due back. Charlie had particularly wanted the fireplace to be finished by the time they returned. Somehow he felt his own personal reputation was at stake, and he couldn't figure out quite what was happening to obstruct him over what should have been a straightforward task.

As a result of his feeling of unease Charlie spent a quiet but somehow unhappy weekend, with a nagging sense of foreboding. He hated things he couldn't explain, and here was something queer which niggled away at his peace of mind. He felt he could not share the worry with his wife, for it touched on his sense of professional ability too nearly, and that had always been a sacred subject in his household.

"There baint nothing in the world my Charlie can't turn 'is 'and to" his wife was fond of saying, while Charlie glowed modestly inside.

On the Monday night, just before bedtime, the Smiths, who lived in the adjacent cottage to the Spendloves, suddenly smelled burning. Mr. Smith got up hurriedly from his comfortable old chair and checked round his own cottage. He could find nothing amiss. He then went outside with a torch. Smoke was coming out of the Spendloves cottage, oozing out of the windows and from around the front door. There was even a column rising from the chimney into the cold night air. There was no sign of a fire, but with some courage Mr Smith took a deep breath and went to the nearest window and peered in. He thought he could make out a faint glow in the centre of the living room, seen through the thick smoke. He hurried back home and rang for the Fire Brigade, communicating a satisfying sense of urgency to the girl on the telephone exchange. He was so glad he had overruled his wife and had the telephone installed, even if it were an extra expense. Now he could point out with justification how valuable it was. Why, they might have been burnt alive in their beds.

Mr. Smith then rang Charlie, to tell him what was happening. Mr. Smith, who worked on the council refuse lorry, thought Charlie was a bit stuck up, and it gave him some satisfaction to rouse the builder from his bed with the bad tidings. Charlie was out of the house in no time, still struggling into his clothes, and he was on the scene long before the Fire Engine, which had to come the seven miles from Newton Abbot. He brought two fire extinguishers along with him, hastily grabbed from the house and workshop, and when he arrived he unlocked the front door, took a deep breath and rushed in, directing the jets of water onto the glowing wood on the floor of the living room. The mantelpiece seemed to be smouldering rather than fully alight, and when the extinguishers ran out Charlie poured a couple of buckets of water over it as well. By the time the brigade arrived the fire seemed to be out, but the mess and smoke made the cottage appear a scene of total desolation. Charlie opened the windows, and the smoke began to clear a bit. The Smiths, from next door, seemed to be enjoying the whole performance immensely!

The firemen were content to check the state of everything, and then leave Charlie on duty to make sure no further outbreak occurred. They returned to welcome and warm beds in Newton, while Charlie sat in an armchair in the wet and smoky living room, with a bucket of water beside him just in case, and in a state of total despair. A large hole had been burned in the wooden floor, about three feet in diameter, and the new mantelpiece which had rested on top of this spot was now burned completely in two, and quite useless. It had been a very nice piece of oak, hard to find, and it had cost a pretty penny. Then Charlie noticed that the stone with the writing on it had slipped endways through the hole in the floor, and it was now standing almost upright, resting on the foundations below. It almost seemed to Charlie that it was mocking him. And the Spendloves would be returning to their home full of happy anticipation later on that day.

Gradually, as Charlie sat there, and the darkness gave way to the bleak dawn of a cold, frosty winter's day, so Charlie's despair was transformed to a fiery, obstinate anger. He would not be beaten. He had never been beaten before. It was that blamed stone which was the cause of all his trouble. He could see it quite clearly now. At first his inclination was to take it outside and smash it to smithereens with the sledgehammer. But in a way that would be to admit further defeat. No, that stone was going to go into the new fireplace, and stay in the new fireplace, or he would know the reason why!

By eight in the morning, when the other two arrived, Charlie had done much of the clearing up, though the smell of smoke still lingered round the cottage. The damaged floor boards had been taken up, and the two halves of the burned mantelpiece carried outside, and hidden round the back. The large stone with the writing on it had been recovered from its resting place, and propped again leaning on the wall, ready to be built into the fireplace in due course. Charlie gave it a malevolent look every time he passed it, daring it to interfere with his plans.

Harry was sent off in the old lorry to get timber for the flooring, a new piece of oak for the mantelpiece, cement, sand and ballast for the new porch foundations, and any more stone he could find for the fireplace. He was to come back by way of Stoneycombe Quarry and bring whatever was available. Charlie delivered his instructions in a tone which was almost harsh, and conveyed the clear message that he had been messed about quite enough on this particular job.

In Harry's absence, Charlie and Bert worked together to finish off the stonework of the fireplace, using the granite that was left as best they could, and filling any gaps with whatever came to hand. It turned out to be the very devil of a job. Charlie swore he could measure by eye exactly how the stone with the writing on it should fit in, but each time they tried it, it was either too large or too small for its intended resting place. The air became very blue as they struggled with the stone for the umpteenth time. The time seemed to fly by without any achievement, and they felt quite exhausted when they had a break at noon for a bite of lunch.

After lunch, fortified by a pint of rough cider each, they tackled the stone with grim determination. Charlie said, between gasps,

"I tell 'e, I'll fix this bluddy stone there if it kills me."

Bert was too out of breath to reply, but he looked rather shocked. At last they got it more or less in place, and after some debate decided to cement it in position. It would not look nearly so good, but they were beyond caring. At any moment the Spendloves might come back, and Charlie was utterly determined that the stone would be firmly in place by the time they turned up. Bert went out into the back yard to mix a bucket or two of cement, and Charlie stood by the fireplace, mopping his brow and refreshing himself with another half pint of cider out of the jar. It had been freezing all day outside, but he felt uncomfortably overheated. Then he heard a noise outside, through the open window, and raised his head to listen. It was the sound of an old fashioned car horn, continuous, and getting louder by the second.

Harry, returning to the village from Stoneycombe after a long and strenuous morning, found the old lorry less than her usual agile self as she crawled very heavily laden indeed up Daignton Hill. The combined load must be as much as Harry had ever carried, he reckoned. He took the road round the south east side of Ipplepen, as that avoided two hills, and set course for his destination. However, he had a very bad fright on Orleigh Hill, the steepest on the route. The brakes on the lorry did not seem to be doing a lot, and it was very fortunate for Harry that he did not meet another vehicle as he careered down the hill, swaying from side to side as he fought with the steering wheel. By the time he came to Poole farm he had lost speed, and was able to take the sharp corner, and start the ascent of the next hill. He wondered whether he ought to have stopped and had a quick look under the lorry to see if he could see anything wrong. If he had done so, he would perhaps have spotted the steady drip of precious brake fluid from a fractured pipe near the master cylinder onto the road.

As it was, he was safely through Poole, and breasting Poole Hill. Now he began to visualise the steep hill down to the village, bordered by cottages, and perhaps a parked car or two at the bottom, before the village main street started. He would stop at the top, and change down into bottom gear, and rely on his engine to hold him. This worked quite well, the hill was mercifully clear, and the old lorry ground its way down, with engine roaring, and the speed only increasing a little. One hill done safely, one to go, or should he risk the main village street and come round the long way? This could involve meeting other vehicles, a farm cart or two, and even the village policeman at this time in the afternoon. At the last minute he swung the lorry left past the farm, and it lurched rather dangerously over to the right on its aged springs. Now Harry was committed to Vicarage Hill, with the cottage, his destination, at the bottom. He was very nearly there.

At the top of the hill he repeated his former procedure. He actually stopped by the Vicarage drive, changed into bottom gear, braced himself, and very gingerly started the descent. He never remembered the old lorry jumping out of gear before, she'd always been very good about that, and Harry was totally unprepared when it happened now, at the most crucial moment. In seconds, on the steepest part of the hill, his speed was up to 50 m.p.h. and more, and he found his brakes were now

31

absolutely useless. He pressed the pedal to the floor and it made no difference. He tried to get back into gear, but she wasn't having any of that. Harry clung with all his strength to the bucking steering wheel, and leaned his elbow on his beloved horn. The noise could be heard all over the peaceful village. He didn't dare think what would happen if he met a vehicle coming up.

Alf Tozer was starting the afternoon collection from the post boxes round the village, driving his little Morris Post Office van. He was slowly climbing Vicarage Hill, in no great hurry for it might still be a bit slippery, when he heard the horn coming down towards him. As the old Bedford lorry careered towards him round the bend still a hundred yards from the bottom, Alf flung his little van into the ditch on the left hand side. Harry, seeing him at the last moment, tried to avoid him by wrenching his wheel to the left, and mounting the bank. He dealt the van a glancing blow only, then the lorry bounced back onto the road, and slid into a patch of ice which always formed there in winter because a spring ran down the bank into the road. Harry had no hope of regaining control, try as he might, and at a speed of a mile a minute the lorry slithered half sideways for twenty yards, then suddenly got a grip on a dry piece of surface, and shot straight through the fence and into the front of Hay Tor Cottage. There was a rending crash like an explosion, and Harry was killed instantly, his chest crushed by the steering wheel. For some strange reason the horn went on sounding, but with a more mournful note.

It was over two hours later that the Fire Brigade chief, who had rushed out with the engine again from Newton Abbot, reckoned it was safe to go into the cottage. They had used what timber they could find, aided by Bert, to shore up the wall round the embedded lorry. Very gingerly they edged their way inside, watched by the horrified Spendloves, who had just arrived, and by Bert, who seemed to be overwhelmed by a sense of resignation. The new chimney breast and fireplace had been totally demolished by the crashing lorry. Instead, there was just a pile of mixed brick and stone rubble, and they dug it away carefully with their hands, looking for Charlie.

"Ee was standing just there afore the fireplace when I last saw un" whispered Bert to no-one in particular.

Charlie was at the bottom of the pile, lying on his back, his head hanging into the hole where the damaged floor boards had been removed. On his chest lay the large stone, the writing uppermost and clearly visible when they cleared the rubble away. Charlie was dead.

THREE. BARNAS'S GHOST.

The shadows danced and flickered in the small chapel, as we sang evensong unaccompanied, to a haunting local chant which I had never heard before, but which seemed to evoke the whole culture and mystery of the Islands. Darkness had fallen with its usual tropical abruptness, and the only source of light was a Tilley pressure lamp, hanging from a beam at the centre of the small building, and by its poor flickering light it was only just possible to follow the words of the Psalm in the well worn pages of the Melanesian Prayer Book.

I stood on my own at a prayer desk, up at the east end of the chapel which was designated as a chancel and sanctuary, although the only feature dividing it from the rest of the chapel was a shallow step with a narrow strip of coconut matting laid along it. The twenty five male students of St. Andrew's Catechist Training College made up the tuneful congregation. None of the three college wives were present, having children to see to at this time of the evening. The lamp light picked out the round beams which supported the leaf roof above,- a roof made of sewn palm leaves from the nearby forest, for the whole chapel, like the surrounding houses, was built of local materials. The chapel had walls which were only three feet high, and so we were open to our surroundings, and our enthusiastic singing competed with the cicadas, whose continuous music would go on far into the night while we all slept.

It was my first term at the college, in fact my first month living in the Solomon Islands, and during that time all my preconceived ideas about being a missionary had been pretty thoroughly shattered. I had been appointed in England to be the deputy warden at Kohimarama College, part of the Diocese of Melanesia, but when we reached Sydney after a pretty ghastly six week sea voyage, it was to find that my "boss-to-be" had suddenly had to leave his work for family health reasons, and return to Australia. As a result I was to be warden and in charge of St. Andrews College as soon as I arrived. At this news we had very nearly turned tail and taken the next flight back to England.

Now, about four weeks before the end of the first term we had spent at the college, I was beginning to get into some sort of routine. I had also had opportunity to get to know the twenty five students in my care, of whom three were married and had families with them. Very fortunately for me, English had to be the main teaching language of the college, and my wife, who is a nurse, was quickly learning pidgin English from the local people, as this was the language spoken by most of the village people around us. Some of their descriptions of their ailments when they attended for treatment were most exotic, if not quite hilarious. My wife often had a job to keep a straight face.

At length Evensong came to an end, we said the final prayers, and I looked forward to our evening meal together, and then some time spent marking answer papers and preparing teaching material for the morrow, - all of which was very new to me, as I had never been a teacher before. I moved through into the small vestry, which was a room partitioned off with a leaf wall from the rest of the chapel, and took off my white cassock and hung it up. This was a welcome activity, as any dressing up in the tropical climate of the Solomons was a penance, and made one feel very sticky. I was about to move back into the chapel, heading for our wooden bungalow a few yards away, when Barnas appeared in the door of the vestry. He stood respectfully silent, but it was obvious he wanted to speak to me.

Barnas came from Malaita, one of the larger islands in the group, and some distance from Guadalcanal, which could be regarded as the "mainland" island, and was where we were based. The Solomon Islanders differed a great deal in racial characteristics, some being very dark and negroid in appearance, while others had lighter skins, and long black hair, and had typical South Sea Islands features. The latter were from the Outer Islands to the east, or even from the Gilbert and Ellice Islands or Polynesia.

Barnas was small in stature, and very dark skinned, with short, black curly hair, and a somewhat wrinkled face which totally concealed his age, - he might have been anything from twenty to forty years old. His lips had the orange colour that comes from chewing a mixture of betel nut and lime, which is some sort of drug. This is a habit not encouraged by the church, but it is universally found throughout the Islands. His teeth, also stained by the betel nut, showed the usual lack of dental care which was also a common feature, and was very obvious when he grinned. Barnas was a quiet and sober citizen in my limited experience, conscientious in his work, and a bit of a loner in some respects. I was later to discover, to my great advantage, that he was not in the least afraid of snakes! But now, standing in the light of the one lamp, clad in the blue shorts and white shirt with badge which were the uniform of the college, he looked a very worried man.

"Is there anything I can do for you, Barnas?" I asked.

He stood first on one leg, then the other. I waited, having learnt over the few weeks that Solomon Islanders are not to be hurried when a weighty matter is at stake.

"Father," said Barnas at length, "I have seen my brother with you in the chapel this night."

I tried to make some sense of this statement, and failed. I was certain that Barnas had no brother in the college, either as a student or as a visitor.

"Where was your brother, Barnas?" I asked, playing for time and somewhat desperately seeking further clues or information.

"He stood beside you in the service, Father" said Barnas very matter-of-factly.

Now I knew quite clearly that I had been on my own in the chancel conducting Evensong, and at least eight feet or so away from the nearest student. There had been no one standing beside me, I was sure, whatever Barnas might say. I peered at him intently, in the dim light. He appeared to be both well and sober. It was out of character that he should make any attempt to pull my leg.

"I have to say, Barnas, that I did not notice your brother at all" I said slowly.

"He stood there, beside you, for many minutes, Father" said Barnas.

I felt totally bewildered. There was a strong temptation to say "Perhaps this is a sign that you are sickening for a bout of malaria fever, Barnas. I suggest you come with me to see my wife and she will give you some tablets." It would be an easy way to evade a situation which I did not understand. I should make a mental note that Barnas could be a little strange at times. But the sight of him standing there so quiet and self assured prompted me to ask one further question.

"Has something like this ever happened to you before, Barnas?" I asked.

"Yes, Father," he replied. "Once I have seen my own father like this but in the church in Honiara."

"When you saw your father, Barnas," I said, "Did it have some special meaning?" I was in rather deep water here, and could feel myself floundering a bit.

"I went at once to my home" said Barnas, very matter-of-factly, and in a quiet voice, "and my father had died of a sudden illness on the very day I had seen him."

I stood in the quietness of the evening, digesting this new information. It all seemed rather strange and far fetched to an European mind, but in the Solomons, in the dim light of the leaf chapel, with the evening music of the cicadas just getting under way in the grass, and the tropical heat around us, who was I to question such a clear and simple statement?

"What do you feel you should do?" I asked him.

"Father, I should like to go now and see my brother and his family"

"Where do they live, Barnas?" I asked. His brother might very well live in Honiara, the capital of the islands, which was quite close by.

"He is living at Suhubassi, Father, on the other coast of Malaita, but it is inland a little bit, on a river," replied Barnas, a little vaguely. This indicated a fairly long and complicated journey, by land and sea, which would take several days, if he was lucky catching a ship when he needed one. If he were unlucky, it could take a couple of weeks. However, we were now not so far off the end of term, and then there would be several weeks of holiday over the Christmas season, so if Barnas went off to see his brother he would not lose too much study time at the college. I knew he was a conscientious student, and that he was up to date with his work.

"Barnas, I think you had better go now and see your brother and his family," I said. "If you pack now I will run you down to the road in the Land Rover, and even though it is evening you may easily get a lift into Honiara."

"Thank you, Father," he replied, and at once went back to his dormitory. A few minutes later we set off, and I duly dropped him down on the road. He set off cheerfully, walking, carrying a shoulder bag, and I hoped he would be lucky with a lift as I drove back up to the college.

To be truthful, with all the varied activity of the College, I almost forget about Barnas in the next two weeks. It was just before the end of the term that I found a letter from him waiting for me when I called into the Diocesan Office in Honiara. Letters in the Solomon Islands do not travel very fast, and I think I was very fortunate to receive it as quickly as I did.

I had to take one of the students in to the Hospital for attention, and so picked up the letter in my pigeon hole. It read: " Dear Father Tyler, I have now come to Suhubassi in safety, and found that to my sorrow my dear brother has indeed died on that day when I have seen him with you in the chapel. I now help my sister, his wife, to plant her garden and re-make her house and then I shall make my return to the college with all my speed. Please give my good wish to your wife and little Andrew, from Barnas." I have to confess that I read the letter several times, and it gave me much food for thought. Here was something which was totally outside all my previous experience of life. It vividly underlined the contrast between what I was experiencing now, in this tropical island scene, and what I had known and found familiar in England, I saw the sea, and the lush green vegetation with a new sense of wonder and respect.

The term drew towards its close with reasonable order and celebration, and on the last day of term, which was a Sunday, and ten days before Christmas Day, I was again conducting evensong in the small college chapel, in the presence of all the students, except Barnas. We sang the office as usual, and then came to the hymn preceding the prayers. It was a favourite, "Fight the good fight" and I knew the words by heart, so did not have to struggle to read them in the dim light. As I sang I glanced to my right in the direction of my congregation of students. They were all there. In fact Barnas was standing beside me. He had no book and he did not sing. Nor did he look at me, but straight in front. He was dressed in ordinary clothes, not his college uniform, and his hands hung motionless by his sides. The words of the hymn froze on my lips. But the rest of the congregation did not seem to be affected in any way whatsoever, and sang the last verse with their customary gusto. I dragged my gaze back to my book, to check that it was indeed the last verse, and then when it finished invited the congregation to kneel in prayer. I glanced sideways again. Barnas was there, standing as still as a statue.

With great difficulty I started leading the prayers, for my mind was in a tumult. I was not really aware of what I was praying for, and meanwhile as I knelt at the prayer desk, Barnas remained standing beside me, motionless. At length I ended the prayers with the familiar words, stood up and moved across in front of the altar. Having bowed before the cross, I turned to face the congregation to give the final blessing. Barnas had gone. I stood as if in a trance, then remembered what I had to do, gave the blessing and knelt, then rose and went into the vestry.

While I was slowly taking my cassock off, Judah came in to collect the snuffer to put out the candles.

"Judah" I said, rather hesitantly, "did you see anyone who was rather unexpected in the chapel tonight?" I was still trying to find some sort of rational explanation for what I had seen, for the alternative was something I didn't want to think about. Perhaps Barnas had indeed returned to the college unexpectedly. Yet I knew that if he had, he would still not have been standing there in the Chapel like that, and dressed in those clothes.

Judah wrinkled his brow in perplexity. He did not really understand my question, which was not surprising, as I didn't really understand it myself.

"I do not think so, Father" he said at length, looking at the ground.

"I thought that someone was standing beside me in the chapel" I said, rather desperately, "but only for a part of our service," I added rather lamely.

Judah looked up, and gave me a rather strange look. "I saw no-one at all, Father" he declared.

Now I knew that Judah had been in the front row of my small congregation that night. If there had been someone standing beside me, Judah could not have failed to see him, at a range of a few yards only. I thanked Judah for his help, and said I must just have been mistaken.

Thank goodness I had Tricia to discuss it all with later that evening. Yet talk about it as we might, it still did not make any logical sense at all. For the rest of the evening, when I should have been tackling a large backlog of work, I could not concentrate on anything but the problem on my mind.

I worked out two facts at length, as I saw them. First, the appearance of Barnas beside me in the chapel meant that he was now, at that moment, in some kind of trouble, if one worked on what I had already learned. Second, the fact that he had appeared to me alone meant that he expected me to do something about the situation. That was where the problem now lay.

In the end I decided, very reluctantly, that the only thing I could do was to go over to Suhubassi, and see what was happening. I knew it was futile to just wait for someone from there to write to me at the college, attractive as this course of action might sound. That was not the way a Solomon Islander in a remote village would act. But if I went off, what would I do with Tricia and Andrew? The college would be more or less closed during the Christmas holiday. I slept very little that night.

The next day there were two minor developments. I discovered that another student at the college, Matthew, also lived on Malaita, and not all that far from Suhubassi. He told me that the village was a days walk from the coast, which is always a rather vague method of measurement, I had found. And then the Blades family, who were wonderful friends from Australia and worked at a large Mission school a few miles up the coastal road, invited us to come and join them over Christmas. In the space of an hour, therefore, I had solved the problem of 'Tricia and Andrew over Christmas, and got myself a guide for the expedition as well. It looked as though I would have to go, for my excuses not to do so were all rapidly evaporating!

I spent the rest of that day making all the necessary arrangements, and finishing off my end of term duties. Luckily I had a student from New Zealand to assist me, and could leave the tidying up of loose ends for him to do. The day after I drove the family along the coast road to Maravovo School, and left them with the Blades family, together with the Land Rover so that they would have their own reliable transport. Jim Blades then drove Matthew and me to Honiara and dropped us off at the Diocesan Office. I had tried to keep my luggage to an absolute minimum, getting all the clothes I needed in that hot climate into one rucksack, but I had agonised over one item. At the last moment I decided to take my rifle with me.

It may sound a little strange to have a missionary with a rifle, but this one had been given to me when I was fourteen, by my father, and it was a very cherished possession. When I had made enquiries in England about including it in my kit, I was assured that it might come in handy for scaring pests away from the crops, and even for doing a little hunting to provide meat for the pot. So with much difficulty at times it had accompanied me on my travels out to the Islands. Now I was reluctant to leave it behind, partly because the local police had read me a long lecture on taking great care of it and never letting it out of my sight, when I had gone to register it, and partly because it was somehow comforting to have something so familiar with me as I set off into the unknown. I did take a Bible with me as well!

In Honiara we had another stroke of luck. The M.V. Selwyn, one of the Diocese of Melanesia ships, was due to leave next day for Auki, on the nearer coast of Malaita. There is a port there, and it is the only town on the island. I booked a passage for myself and Matthew, and then went to organise a room in the Diocesan rest house, while Matthew arranged to stay with "won-toks" – people from his area who spoke the same language as he did. There are thirty four different languages spoken in the Solomons, and those from the same language area always offer hospitality to one another like members of an extended family.

That night I felt very lonely and uncertain. Was I really doing the right thing? Had I interpreted the message I had been given in the right way? It seemed hard to have to leave my wife and son "in a strange land" just before the festival of Christmas.

Matthew arrived early next morning, after I had eaten a rather sketchy breakfast, and we went aboard the Selwyn at 8.a.m. She sailed soon after, fairly crammed with cheerful passengers going to their homes for Christmas. I had always considered myself to be a good sailor, with lots of boating experience as a boy. On the liner Australis, I had been unaffected by both violent pitching and rolling of the ship in very bad weather as we travelled from the Straits of Gibralter all the way to Sydney. An hour on the sixty foot long Selwyn soon revealed my seaworthiness limitations to me, and to everyone else on board! I retired below to a very small bunk, feeling very ill. I did come up on deck briefly as we passed down the channel between the halves of Gela Island, and put down passengers at Siota, but I then retired below in a hurry as we started to cross the rough sea to Malaita. I was very relieved three hours later when I was told that Auki was in sight, and I staggered up on deck, and watched as we chugged the last half mile into Auki harbour in the evening light, taking deep breaths of wonderful fresh air.

Auki looked like every other Melanesian settlement, with a few white houses, many more leaf houses, a small quay and a few sheds, and a lot of coconut palms. Behind were the usual hills carpeted in thick forest.

I spent that night in the Diocesan rest house, eating some of the iron rations Tricia had provided me with, and not at all comfortable on a very utilitarian bed. The next morning Matthew arrived with two companions, and a debate ensued on how best to get to Suhubassi. Matthew said we could go round the coast by boat, but he did not know of any boat which might be going that way. A canoe, he said, could be rather dangerous because of the very rough waters near the end of the Island. I did not in the least like the sound of any more rough waters, especially in a canoe, and asked what the alternative was. He said we could go along the coast road as far as Fauabu, where the mission hospital was located, and then turn inland, and walk through the bush.

"How long will that take, Matthew?" I asked.

"Probably two, three days, father" he replied. Probably two at his walking pace, I reflected, and three at mine!

At that point I glanced round and saw the Archdeacon of Malaita, Peter, loading his ancient Dodge truck with rations down at the quayside, which had been brought over on the Selwyn. I walked down to have a word with him, - we had met once before in Honiara, and he told me he was taking most of the supplies along the road to the hospital at Fauabu. I asked if we could beg a lift, and he was delighted to help, so I returned to Matthew and the others and told them I had decided on the land route, and that we should begin in a few minutes with a lift on Peter's truck to Fauabu. I then discovered that Matthew's two friends were to be part of the expedition. This was a characteristic feature of Solomon Islander's behaviour, - the ability to drop everything, work, family, gardening, and just take off on an expedition for a few days, or a week or two! They could always count on hospitality in villages they might pass through, or live off the land. They obviously felt it was far more interesting to be part of a strange and inexperienced Europeans retinue, than working in boring old gardens. They eyed my rifle, carried by Matthew, with excitement, and seemed convinced that hunting or something even more daring was on the menu.

The ride down the Malaita coast road in Archdeacon Peter's old truck was exciting and memorable! Peter drove, and his lovely Polynesian wife, and two of their children travelled in the cab. I was kindly offered a seat, but insisted on travelling on the back, where I could clutch onto the back of the cab. There were some sacks of flour we could sit on, but most of the time it was less painful to stand up. The lorry bounded down the dirt road leaving a cloud of swirling yellow dust behind it, and every now and then charged across a simple wooden bridge, with no sides, which spanned a gully or a stream. At a distance the bridges looked far too narrow for the lorry to cross, and indeed there were only inches to spare, but the driver knew them all very well indeed, and judged them to perfection. (On a later occasion I drove the lorry myself, and did not judge one of them nearly so well, but that is another story!)

We reached Fauabu before noon, and having helped unload part of the cargo from the lorry, we were given refreshments by Sister Helen, the matron. Cool lime juice was a wonderful tonic in the heat of the day. I declined an offer of lunch, however, and declared that we ought to set off so as to get as far as possible before dark. Tropical night descends very suddenly about six in the evening. Matthew reappeared, this time with three more companions to add to the earlier two, so my total retinue came to six! There was some discussion about who should carry what, and then we set off, after I had made sure that the rifle was not loaded and that I was personally carrying all the ammunition. Matthew carried the rifle to start with, but I could see that the position of gun-bearer would be much sought after.

We climbed away from the hospital and the adjacent sea, until we reached a ridge which was open, and gave a wonderful view back, with Gela in the distance across the strait. There were no ships in sight. Then we turned and plunged into the thick bush, and all views ceased abruptly. We stumbled along a very narrow and muddy path, which twisted around the large trees, and tried to follow the contours of the hills. Not with a lot of success, it has to be said, as we always seemed to be going up or down hill. Going up I was sometimes reduced to hands and knees, and going down I ended up on my bottom more often than not. We came to junctions with other paths every mile or so, and I hoped that Matthew and his Malaita friends really did know the right path to follow. I could not see any signs or landmarks, and they all seemed just the same to me.

Once during the afternoon we descended into a steep valley, and found a bridge over the small river running along the bottom. The bridge was a single rough hewn tree trunk, resting on each bank, and the drop below it was a good twenty feet. The Islanders skipped across it without a second thought. I moved across it very gingerly, trying hard not to look at the rushing water and boulders beneath me. The forest was surprisingly quiet, with few bird calls, but always the noise of dripping water. It was also totally shaded, the canopy of trees above making it hardly possible for any rays of sunlight to penetrate. We seemed to be the only inhabitants, until I felt something bite my foot, - I had taken my sandals off as they were worse than useless in the slippery mud. I hopped about, registering my discomfort loudly, until the pain began to work off a bit. Meanwhile my retinue all surrounded me, saying "Sorry, Father" at frequent intervals, as though they were responsible for biting me! It turned out I had put my big foot on a procession of large black ants which had been crossing our path at that point, and they had signified their extreme displeasure in the way which came very naturally to them. I looked much more carefully where I was putting my feet from then on, but even so I got bitten several more times.

Fifteen Love

We came at dusk to a village called Honae, and here we met a strange procession. A woman, suffering from post-natal bleeding, was being taken down to the hospital at Fauabu on a stretcher. I did not see her, for she was covered with a strip of matting, but I wondered how on earth the four bearers would make it over the tree trunk bridge we had crossed, as well as the rest of the narrow slippery path. However, they all seemed very confident and cheerful, as did the nurse from the hospital who was in charge of the operation, and who was carrying the new-born baby.

The village was built in the usual type of clearing, and later in the evening I joined the villagers in their chapel for evening prayers, led by their village catechist. I did not understand any of the service, which was conducted in their local language, and there were no books available for the congregation.

Supper followed some time later, and this consisted of a "soup soup" in which I thought I detected some chicken. But one could not be sure, and one could hardly see what one was eating in the darkness, which may have been just as well. The first time I had "soup soup" I thought it was local chicken, and it turned out to be opossum! The mixture was accompanied by huge lumps of Kumera, the local sweet potato of the islands, which was hard to swallow and pretty indigestible! It gave me a great yearning for ordinary potatoes every time I met it. Finally, I was given a couple of small bananas, which were a great relief! The night was spent on a wooden slatted bed, with a rather rough rug for company. It was very hot and humid, and the local mosquitoes sensed a very pleasant change from their usual diet. Even though theoretically protected from Malaria by the drugs we took weekly, I did not enjoy being bitten. The mosquitoes and I had an equally restless night!

In the morning I requested just fruit for breakfast, having glimpsed something that looked suspiciously like the previous nights "soup soup" which was ready to make a repeat appearance. I then went in search of the village toilet facilities. To this day I cannot be sure whether I found them, but then improvisation has to be second nature for jungle explorers!

We set off by 8.30.a.m. and were immediately swallowed up by a jungle path identical to the day before. All day we followed it, the only respite being when we came to a small river with a stony beach beside it on a bend. Here I called a halt, and we ate our lunch, such as it was. We paddled our tired and muddy feet in the cool water, and I decided to swap my shorts for swimming trunks, as being the most practical garment when I was constantly falling down and getting wet and muddy. We plodded on through the long hot afternoon, with everyone having to go at my slow pace, and then as it was beginning to get dark, Matthew and his friends stopped and held a conference. I could not understand what they were saying, but Matthew explained to me that by now we should have reached the village which was our destination, and as we had not done so, then we must be lost. Which conclusion was totally logical, but not much comfort to a very weary and footsore traveller.

We came soon to a slightly larger river, and the company decided that we should construct a shelter of branches and leaves, and camp there for the night. Remembering the "luxuries" of civilisation on the previous night, I have to admit with shame that the prospect of a night camping in the bush did not appeal to me at all! However, before construction had begun, one of my retinue noticed a branch floating down the river, which had obviously been cut from a tree very recently. This, we agreed, suggested that someone must be further up the river to have cut it off. And if someone, perhaps a village full of someones? We began to make our way upstream, hopping from rock to rock, or wading in the cool water. At length, after about an hour, and when it had really become pitch dark, we spotted a fire and the dim outlines of some houses on a ridge above the river. They were a very welcome sight, and we were given a warm greeting and caringly looked after as we had been the night before. I slept much better, through sheer exhaustion, I think, and was comforted by the assurance from Matthew that we should definitely reach Suhubassi on the following day.

"It is really not far to travel now, Father" he promised.

I had learned by this time not to get too excited by such a prophecy, but I was hopeful. We pushed on next day, through identical country, though always climbing a bit, it seemed to me, until in the afternoon we crossed a ridge and through the trees glimpsed out destination below us, and still some miles away. Moreover, beyond the village and its gardens, and to our left, we could also see the sea, stretched out to the horizon. It was a very reassuring sight for me, at least. The village again stood on a low ridge, but this time the river below it was larger, being a lot nearer to the sea. To our right the river seemed to emerge from a fairly steep gorge, with cliff like sides in places, but below the village it widened and deepened, though the far bank was still pretty steep. There was a long deep pool, about a quarter of a mile long, before more rapids, and the river passed on through dense forest to the sea.

We received a great welcome in Suhubassi, and somehow I got a strange feeling that we were indeed expected, and came in the guise of deliverers. However, much as I looked around me, there was no sign of Barnas. We were ushered into a larger leaf house, which it turned out belonged to the village Catechist, and given some coconut milk to drink. There was a natural constraint, and at length I had to pluck up courage and say

"I have come to you to see if I can help Barnas." Matthew, who was acting as interpreter, translated for the villagers.

There was a long, sad silence, and then the Catechist spoke. He spoke for a long time, and I could tell by the expression on his face that it was bad news. At length he stopped, and Matthew repeated his story for me:

"Father" he said, "we are most sad to have to tell you that Barnas is dead. We are in great trouble in our village here. As you see, we have below us a beautiful river, which is a great help to us, but a few months ago it was the scene of a great sorrow. A young woman of our village was washing her clothes in the river, as is our custom, when a great crocodile suddenly seized her. Another woman, her companion and friend, has seen this animal at the same moment, and it is truly an enormous beast. Since then we have taken great care, but even so this animal has killed two of our women and a large child. The child was the child of the brother of Barnas, and he was so angry that he armed himself with his bush knife, and went down to the river, and sought to take his revenge when he could see the crocodile, but when it came and he fought very bravely with it, it still killed him easily by dragging him beneath the river, and we saw him no more.

Then after a few days Barnas came to us, and we sat for many hours and prayed and talked about what we should do. We made a food for the crocodile with one of our goats, to bring it to the beach, and we all helped Barnas to prepare his spears. Then in the evening he went down to the river, with a lamp to give him some light. On the second night of waiting, the crocodile came, and Barnas drove a spear into him, but the crocodile is very tough and strong, and his skin is thick. He came back, and as Barnas threw his second spear his foot slipped on the muddy bank, and he fell upon the beast. Barnas then tried to fight it with his knife, and we all ran to his help, but the beast was too strong for us, and it dragged Barnas beneath the waters. We have never seen him again, and we weep for him. Now we hardly dare go down to the river, even for water, for we have seen the beast again and it is very much alive."

I sat and listened to this story with mounting sorrow and apprehension. I knew that the local crocodile, the Fijian species, can grow to thirty feet in length, and I also knew that every now and then one develops a taste for human flesh, and becomes a regular man eater. Perhaps as they grow older, they find it harder to catch their natural prey, and women washing in a large river are easy pickings. Anyway, such creatures bring incredible strength and cunning to their hunting tactics. Only a year before, a party of missionaries in a large native canoe had been attacked at the mouth of a river, and they had had a lucky escape when one of their number bravely beat off the crocodile with her umbrella. She saved their lives, but the umbrella was never the same again!

Now, it seemed, I would have to make the acquaintance of one such monster, for it was very obvious that the villagers saw my arrival as expressly for the purpose of ridding them of this scourge. I decided that some reconnaissance, while there was still daylight, was the best way to make a start. Some of the men of the village had gone off hunting in the bush, but the Catechist and members of my own party accompanied me down the winding path to the river. I did take my rifle with me, to improve morale, and put several rounds in the magazine to boost my own courage.

As we had seen from above, the river emerged from the gorge into the long pool, which had a pebbly beach at that point, and Matthew explained to me that the villagers used this pool for everything, so to speak. At the top end, water for drinking and cooking was taken out, using hollow bamboo trunks as containers. Then came the washing and bathing area, and then the section for the washing of clothes was downstream. Finally, furthest downstream, and close to the forest, the river provided flush sanitation which I did not wish to investigate too closely, and especially if there was a very large crocodile as an audience. The women had all been attacked while washing their clothes in that part of the river. I gathered that washing and bathing had now become rare pastimes among the villagers. I looked out across the fifty yard pool to the cliff beyond. The water was perfectly still, with hardly a ripple.

"What time of day does the crocodile usually come?" I asked.

Matthew consulted and told me "usually in the early morning, or perhaps at dusk, Father."

"We will go back to the village and work out a plan," I said, looking again out over the calm pool. It was hard to believe that such murderous danger could be lurking beneath its surface.

That night we talked together, and pooled our abilities. I was more than ever pleased that I had brought my rifle with me, yet I did not have a lot of confidence in its power, - it was only a .22 weapon, though I did have high velocity bullets for it. Even if I managed to hit the crocodile, would I do more than tickle it up a bit? The thought of a wounded croc rampaging round the village with its flimsy houses didn't bear thinking about. Supper was served and we settled down to a somewhat sombre meal, by the light of two old hurricane lamps. As I stared down at my soup-soup, I suddenly saw a small fox-like face staring back at me. I started, and turned to Matthew,

"What on earth is it?" I asked urgently, and in a whisper.

"It is just a flying fox, Father" he replied.

"What is that?" I asked, none the wiser.

Matthew seemed at a loss. "It flies in the night, mainly," he explained, "and it eats the fruit of the kapok tree which we use for filling our pillows."

I had to start eating, as my kind hosts were watching me and waiting for me to start sampling this great treat. It tasted a bit rank, but alright, and I later discovered that it was a giant fruit-eating bat, harvested by the villagers from a cave they knew of in the gorge above the river. I went to bed and slept very fitfully, listening to the noises of the night. There was an endless chorus of frogs down by the river, to rival the cicadas, and then the strange rasping clicking noise of the flying foxes, which at first I thought was the noise of a troupe on monkeys until I remembered that they do not have any monkeys in the Solomons.

I got up early at first light, and grasping my rifle made my way quietly down to the pool again. In the morning light, with a little mist over it, it looked sinister and still. Suddenly I nearly jumped out of my skin as a voice said "There is nothing there this morning yet, Father," from a bush three feet away from me. Matthew had had the same idea as me, but had got to his hiding place first. I could not feel very surprised, as my hope that the crocodile would be lying on the surface waiting for me to take pot shots at it was not in truth very likely.

After breakfast we held a council of war. I decided to ask for a small leaf shelter to be built on the beach at the clothes washing place. It should be three sided, and open to the river, but with two wooden bars set horizontally across the open river side, so that I could rest my rifle as I fired, if need be. It should also have a rough seat, and a place to stand a lamp safely. The lamp should be covered with some sort of tin, so that its light would be hidden until I wanted it.

Matthew translated my instructions, and the villagers scurried off to carry them out. There was a general sense of excitement and optimism, now that something was going to be done. I desperately hoped that it was not misplaced, as some seemed to see me as a sort of divine messenger sent to right a great wrong.

I rested during the heat of the day in my house, and it was as usual desperately hot and humid. In the early afternoon I got up and went down to see how the work was progressing. The shelter, made of kapok branches and thatched with leaf, was a work of art. It stood about three yards from the edge of the river, at the head of the small beach. Matthew proudly showed me a modification they had thought up.

"Father, if you need to leave the shelter with quickness," he said, "you just turn and push on this part at the back, and it will easily fall down."

I thanked him very much, and tried not to think of the circumstances which would lead to me leaving the shelter with quickness! Later in the afternoon, two brave women from the village washed their clothes in the river, while I stood guard with my rifle at the ready. By doing this I hoped to entice the crocodile to come up river, for I guessed that it spent most of its time down where the river flowed into the sea. These particular reptiles were sea going creatures. I figured that the scent of the clothes being washed would be carried down to it by the current.

I had an early supper, avoiding soup soup, and being fortified with some of my precious iron rations as well, and took up my position in the shelter, with my rifle across my knees, loaded and cocked. From time to time, as it grew dark, I sighted the rifle across the pool. I soon realised that I could see very little through its telescopic sight. The hours passed very slowly, the frogs and bats serenaded me, and the mosquitoes feasted off me. I did not even dare to take evasive action against the little blighters! Soon after midnight the lamp went out, its supply of paraffin exhausted. My seat grew harder and harder, and my posterior more and more tender. The pool, seen dimly, remained still and untroubled. Sometime after midnight I suddenly realised it was Christmas Day.

Every now and then I think I dozed for a few minutes, but not for long. At length the dawn came, and even though I felt like death warmed up, I forced myself to be more alert. This was one of the most likely times in the day. I kept watch until the first villagers appeared, and then got up and made my way very stiffly back to the village. I said to Matthew

"I shall go to sleep, now, and then perhaps we could have a
Christmas Communion Service in the small leaf village
chapel?"

Matthew thought this a very good idea, and went off to discuss
it with the village Catechist. Then I went to the house allocated
to me, collapsed on the bed, and slept. Fortunately there were
not many mosquitoes about during the day.

I planned to keep watch again the next night, so slept as long
as I could. Meanwhile two women went through the clothes
washing routine again, watched over by Matthew with my rifle.
I was woken by the empty shell case which served as a bell
being rung, and went over to the chapel. It was sadly a very
sombre Christmas service. Somehow the traditional readings
seemed out of place, and though we sang several of the
Christmas carols it was difficult to feel a great sense of joy.

After an early supper I took up my position once again in the
shelter. I think it was about 9.p.m. when I heard a soft swirl in
the water in front of me. In a second my senses were fully alert,
mainly stimulated by fear. A few yards out in the pool there
was something which looked darker than the surrounding
water. Very carefully I raised my rifle, and looked through the
sight. I could see nothing. A telescopic sight reduces light at
the best of times, and these conditions were the worst possible.
I would have to try using the original open sights on the rifle. I
gingerly lowered the rifle, and twisted the holding clamps on
top of the barrel. As I did so I suddenly remembered that it was
years since I had used the open sights, and the chance of them
still being accurate was very poor. The telescopic sight slid off
noiselessly, and I placed it on my seat. Again I raised the rifle,
and peered through the aperture of the back sight. I could pick
out the dark shadow now, but was it the head of a crocodile or
just a trick of the light. For what seemed an age I stared at it,
until my eyes ran. I could not afford to make a mistake, for I
reckoned I would only have the one chance.

To this day I cannot remember what I saw then. Perhaps it was a slight movement in the water, perhaps a trick of the light, like the reflection of a star on a small ripple. Anyway, I made up my mind, aimed vaguely at the centre of the "lump" and squeezed the trigger. The echo of my shot reverberated round the cliffs and gorge, hugely magnified. I reloaded at once, by instinct, and pulled the piece of tin off my lamp. I stood up, holding the lamp in one hand, and my rifle in the other, and stared out across the dark water. There was nothing.

Then, without any warning, a huge head appeared out of the pool straight in front of me, with water cascading off it, and by the feeble light of the lamp I saw two evil looking yellow eyes, and a vast mouth full of teeth. It was so large, and so near to me, I dropped the lamp in fright. If I could have turned and run, I should have done so, but I had totally forgotten about Matthew's secret panel. I could hear the cries of the villagers, woken by my shot, and hurrying down the path. Instinctively I aimed my rifle as though it was a shotgun, without using the sights, and fired another shot at point blank range.

I continued reloading and firing, while the monster stood partly out of the water and seemed to sway to and fro, and then there was a click, and I knew my magazine was empty. This sobered me a little, and I hastily reached into my pocket for my spare magazine, and slotted it into place with trembling fingers. I now had five more bullets, only.

The lamp had smashed, but the leaking paraffin on the beach had caught fire, and by the light of these flames I saw the crocodile sliding back into the water, its jaws snapping and tail lashing. Now I took a more careful aim, and shot it three times between the eyes. It was hard hit, and after a time it grew still, and I became aware of a group of people in the shadows behind me. It seemed that the entire village population was there, men, women and children. For a full minute, I guess, we all stood in silence and looked at the dead beast, while I kept it covered

56

with my rifle just in case it was pretending to be dead. It no longer moved at all, and so I climbed out of the shelter, slowly relaxing. Three or four of the men, carrying spears and knives, came to stand beside me. Matthew bent down, and taking a leaf from the shelter, held it to the burning paraffin. Then, as though it was somehow a symbolic gesture, he applied it to my shelter, which quickly caught fire. By this flaming light the scene was well illuminated, and I suddenly remembered my telescopic sight, and lurched towards the shelter just in time to recover it off the seat.

Matthew said "Sorry Father, I did not realise a piece of your gun was there." I took back my rifle which I had thrust into his hands before my rescue mission.

"All is well now, thank God" I said, and meant it.

Then a rope was brought, and two of the village men waded rather gingerly into the river and wound it round the crocodile's forelegs, and then came out quite quickly with the rope ends. As it became apparent that the beast was truly dead, a mood of relief, confidence and celebration rapidly developed, with many hands helping to pull on the rope. I personally felt sick with relief and anti-climax, and said I would now go and rest in my house. I was not very anxious to see what they did with the crocodile at that time of night, but as I stumbled back up the path to the village I pondered the ethical position of eating something that not long ago had itself devoured your nearest and dearest. Cannibalism had only died out a couple of decades ago, and this could be rather the same, I felt, but one step removed. I resolved, as I dragged myself into the house, to be careful what I ate on the morrow! It was not surprising that I did not sleep at all well.

I should like to record that the next day was spent in thanksgiving and celebration. For the villagers, it was, I believe, and I could hear it going on for much of the day, with the village drum and "bell" in constant use. However, I went down with mild Malaria, and spent three days tossing and turning, and dosing myself with the Cloroquin tablets which a careful wife had sent with me. It was a further three days before I was strong enough to start the journey home, with my faithful company led by Matthew. For him it became quite an epic saga, I believe, and lost nothing in the telling!

The crocodile measured about twenty six feet long, but the only souvenir I have to remember it by is one very sharp tooth. Luckily for me, I never sampled the full set!

FOUR.   ONE ROOM AT THE INN.
A DIFFERENT CHRISTMAS STORY.

He lifted the latch with some difficulty, and then leant against the old oak door. To his intense relief it opened, though it creaked in protest. This was his third stroke of luck, he thought. First, because he had been driving so slowly in the atrocious conditions he had actually spotted the Inn, set back a little from the road, but hardly visible beneath its coating of snow. He had also spotted its old "Accommodation" sign as he crawled past in the car. And second, he had seen the deep snowdrift blocking the road before he had actually ploughed into it. True, because a second drift had made the road so narrow he had not dared try to turn round, and he did not fancy reversing back along the rapidly vanishing road, with no visibility to speak of. After sitting in the car for a few minutes, and watching the snow swirling past the windows, he grabbed his small overnight bag, got out of the car quickly, locked it, and headed back down the road with the collar of his coat turned up. He had to trudge through ever deepening snowdrifts, while the biting wind took his breath away, but he reached the Inn at last, and the door now opened for him.

The door opened into quite a spacious entrance hall, panelled in dark oak. David at once noticed two things. Despite the sudden shutting out of that biting wind, there was no feeling of snug comfort and warmth inside the Inn. Also, the only light came from an old hurricane lantern, placed on top of the counter on the far side of the room. He paused for a few seconds, looking round, and then moved slightly reluctantly across to the counter. On the counter beside the lantern stood an old bell, of the kind which has a spring loaded clapper attached underneath the bell itself. David felt he didn't really want to ring it, for he was fearful of waking up the entire household. He glanced at his watch, and noted that it was just past eleven.

He took a deep breath, and picked up the bell and rang it, quite gently. The strident ringing echoed all round the largely empty entrance hall. Nothing happened at all, so after a couple of minutes he plucked up courage and rang it again, twice, for good measure. A slight feeling of unease stole over him.

Suddenly, and with no preliminary warning, a door in the wall behind the counter opened. An old man stood there, carrying a candle, which he held aloft and which illuminated his face, revealing white hair and a long white beard, and also a pair of bright eyes beneath craggy eyebrows. He wore a pair of rimless spectacles, perched on a large nose which seemed to owe its colour to much sampling of the stock in the inn cellar. As David looked at this person with interest, there was a sound behind him, and as he swung round he saw the front door opening slowly. For a moment he feared it had blown open because he had not latched it properly. But it was not so. A woman appeared in the doorway, struggled to shut the door behind her, and then stood still, gasping a little. Like David she too wore a coat, though not a very substantial one, and had her coat collar turned up. She had a scarf round her head, and she clutched a handbag. Small deposits of snow detached themselves from her clothing and dropped to the floor.

"Yerss?" said the old man, and David swung round again to face him. Now he noticed that mine host was dressed in what appeared to be a long retired army greatcoat, and he wore a flat cap slightly askew on his head, above the white hair. His manner could not be described as very friendly, but, David thought, that was perhaps only to be expected in the circumstances, and he was probably not expecting any visitors at that time of night.

"Could you let me have a room for the night, please?" he asked.

The old man looked at him, and seemed to consider his reply.
"Just the one room left" he declared at length. "Number three."
He turned and peered at the key board behind him, lifting the candle to give more light. "Can't see a bloomin thing" he muttered. "Electricity's been off since first thing this morning. Wires is all down. There'll be no breakfast" he added encouragingly. He reached up and took the last key off its hook on the board, and then turned and put it on top of the counter. He then fumbled around beneath the counter, out of sight, and produced two candles and a candle holder. A further search in his pockets turned up a battered box of matches.

   David was aware of a movement behind him.

 "Did I hear you say that was the last room available?" asked a clear, rather musical voice. There was almost a hint of panic in the question.

 "The old man looked at her over the top of his ancient spectacles.
"Just the one double room" he muttered. "First floor," he added as an afterthought, "bathroom at the end of the corridor. Bain't no hot water, o' course" he concluded by way of encouragement. Then he turned, opened the door behind him and went slowly out, carrying his candle.

 David turned to the woman. "Are you stuck in the snow as well?" he asked.

 "Yes" she replied, "I'm trying to get home to Hellerby. "I think I may have passed your car when I clambered through that last snowdrift. I was a fool to go out today at all, but my mother has not been well, and I suddenly felt I must get over to see her and take her a few things for Christmas. She lives all on her own."

 David glanced sideways at the single key lying on the counter by his hand. The whole situation was certainly most awkward, and he did not feel up to resolving it so late at night.

"Do you happen to know if there is another place with accommodation anywhere near?" he asked her.

She said, rather bleakly, "I don't think there's anywhere within five miles, at least, in either direction." Her voice no longer had its musical quality, and she sounded very tired, almost defeated. She had not removed her head scarf, and she seemed almost poised ready for flight. Outside, the wind threw a flurry of sleet against the windows by way of variation. David thought "No room at the Inn. Where have I heard that one before?"

He said "Look, one thing is quite certain. Neither of us is going out in that sort of bitter weather again tonight. It would be utterly foolhardy. There must be some sort of lounge here with a sofa I can make use of." He moved across the hall to the only other door and tried it. It was locked.

She shivered a little. "Look," she said, "We'd better go upstairs and see what we can find. At least it may be a little warmer up there." David took the box of matches, struck one, and lit a candle, which he put in the holder. Then, with the candle in one hand, and his bag in the other, he led the way to the stairs. The woman picked up the other candle, the matches and the one key, and followed him. The stairs were old and creaked a lot, and after a right turn brought them to a small upper landing, with a corridor running off it. A strip of matting had been laid on the bare boards. David lifted up his candle, and managed to read the figure one painted on the first door they came to. They moved slowly down the corridor.

"He said it was a double room" said David quietly. "It's sure to have twin beds, they always do." He suddenly felt very very tired. The prospect of a bed, any kind of bed, had become desperately appealing.

They found room number three, and she fitted the key into a type of Yale lock, and turned it. David reached for the latch and opened the door, then stretched out to find the light switch before he remembered that the power was off, and the only light was his candle. He lifted up the candle, and they both looked round. The room was small, and sparsely furnished. It had a small wardrobe, an upright chair, a table, a bedside cabinet, and one standard size double bed. David looked at it in dismay.

"I'll have to go and look somewhere else" he muttered, and despite his best endeavours a note of dejection and defeat sounded in his voice. The woman stood in thought for a few seconds, then she seemed to come to a decision, for she removed her scarf and shook her hair.

"I think that's silly" she said. "If all the other rooms are occupied, there is no-where else to go, and you can't go waking other people up in the middle of the night."

"I could try the bathroom, with a blanket."

"Well, if you try sleeping in the bathroom what happens if someone else wants to use it during the night? They might not want an audience" she added, giving him a slightly mischievous look which he failed to see. He did now look at her, slightly surprised, and saw that without her scarf the candle light revealed a mass of dark brown hair framing an attractive rounded face. She wore little make up, and her long coat hid what he guessed was a slim figure, which went with her medium height. She did not appear to be aware of his scrutiny. He judged her to be a few years younger than himself, say in her mid-thirties.

"I could sleep in that chair" he said, trying and failing to convince either of them.

"You most certainly couldn't" she said. "You'd be on the floor in no time." For the first time he thought he detected a twinkle in her eyes. "Anyway, I doubt it would support your weight, by the look of it, and if you snored in the night, there is no way I could reach you to kick you!"

There was no doubt about the twinkle in her eye, now, and her voice had recovered its musical quality. There was even a faint suggestion that she was enjoying the adventure.

David laughed. "Well" he said, "I suppose we shall have to make the best of a bad job." As soon as he said it he realised what an ungallant statement it was, and floundered around, while she gave him a sideways look.

"It's lucky I thought of bringing along my bag with me from the car," he managed. "At least I have got my night things here."

"Lucky old you" she retorted, and she was smiling again. "I've only got a spare handkerchief with me."

He was at once concerned. "You're very welcome to my pyjamas."

She said "Thank you, kind sir. Do you think we could share them? You are a lot taller than I am, so you could keep the bottoms, and I could take out a loan on the top half."

David rummaged in his bag, and produced his very old dressing gown, and the rather lurid set of orange pyjamas. He also produced a pair of much worn slippers.

"Everything is now revealed!" he declared, rather like a second rate and partially successful conjurer, trying to cover his embarrassment. He handed the pyjama top to her. Then, seeking to make the situation easier for them both he said

"Why don't you go down to the bathroom first, and then when I follow you, you can be getting into bed?" She smiled at him, and gave him a grateful look. It was a warm and friendly smile, he noted. She took the spare candle and lit it, and put it in a holder on the table. Then she took it and moved to the door.

"Don't get lost," said David. "He said it was down at the end of the corridor."

David changed into his half pyjamas and the old dressing gown, and was waiting for her when she returned.

"Last door on the right" she told him, "and freezing cold. Someone had left the window partly open. I tried to shut it, but it wouldn't budge. No sign of any soap, either."

"See you later, I hope" said David cheerfully, and set off on his own journey. The whole night had an air of complete unreality, he thought as he walked cautiously down the passageway, lit by his candle. Was he really going to share a bed with a total stranger of the opposite sex? And what if she made accusations about him in the future? They didn't even know one another's names! And yet what else could he have done? He found the bathroom door, with "bath" painted on it in crude lettering. It was even colder in there than she had described it.

Any other course of conduct would have seemed truly unkind, even brutal. How could he have said to her "Well, I got here first, so you'll have to make your own arrangements." He resolved not to be parted from any of his clothing, but just to clean his teeth. He wondered how she had managed. How long had he been in the bathroom, and how much time would she need to get into bed?

He decided to count fifty, slowly. That must be enough time. She didn't look like a girl who would take ages spraying herself with things. Anyway, it was too cold for messing about. Where had he got to with his counting? He began again. It reminded him of childhood games of hide and seek. Only this time he wasn't seeking anything, except a warm, comfortable bed. And would she be hiding, and what should he do if she had changed her mind. Even locked him out?

He carefully opened the bathroom door, and slowly and quietly made his way up the corridor by the light of his flickering candle. The door was open, and inside the bedroom, by the light of two candles, she was revealed half sitting up in the bed, the pyjama jacket very inadequately buttoned. He suddenly remembered with horror that he had been meaning to sew on those two missing buttons for ages, but had just not got round to it. It was the problem when one no longer had a wife to look after you. He felt embarrassed, but decided to pretend that he had not noticed.

"Mission accomplished?" she asked. Was it his imagination, or did she suddenly look tired and a little frightened?

"Are you quite sure you don't mind me coming in there with you?" he asked, suddenly wanting to give her an escape clause.

"Come on" she replied, "You'll catch your death of cold out there if you haver about any longer."

He took off the old dressing gown and spread it on the bed. She noticed the dark hair on his chest. He slid into the bed, keeping as near to the edge as possible without actually falling onto the floor.

"Candles out now?" he asked, and for reply she leaned over and blew hers out on the bedside table. He had placed his candle on the chair, and could just reach it. The room was plunged into darkness.

"Goodnight, and I do hope that you sleep well" he whispered.

"The same to you" she replied in her soft voice. "I just hope that Father Christmas doesn't disturb us!" He had completely forgotten that it was Christmas night. He lay by the edge of the bed for some time, trying to will himself to go to sleep. He was not comfortable, and the bed was cold. He did not dare move for fear of disturbing her. Anyway, he had nowhere to go but onto the floor! Presently he became aware of a slight fluttering movement in the bed. He tried to work out what it was, without success. At length he whispered "Are you awake still?"

"Yes" came the reply out of the darkness.

"Are you alright?" he asked solicitously.

"I think I'm too cold to get to sleep" she replied. "I have a lovely heated blanket at home."

"Would you like my dressing gown?" he enquired.

"No, thank you" came the reply from the dark. Then, softly

"I could do with a hug, I think."

Slightly stunned, David reached out his right hand, and encountered her shoulder, encased in his pyjama top. It was the first time he had touched her. For a few moments she let his hand rest there. Then she turned towards him, and his hand slid over her shoulder and down her back. He moved across the cold centre of the bed, and suddenly she was pressed against him, her head nestling in his shoulder. He drew her closer, and could feel her shivering. He tightened his arm against her back, and tried to pass on what heat he could muster, which was not very much. Over a period of five minutes or so she stopped shivering, and nestled even closer to him.

He thought "we can sleep alright like this" and began trying to do so. But then she moved her leg a little, so that her knee rubbed against his. A small, tingling shock moved up his leg, and for the first time he thought "what happens if I become aroused? What on earth will she think of me, and what will happen then?" Yet there was no way he could disengage himself now.

As if to answer his unspoken question, she again moved a little in the bed. Her thighs moved against his, and at the same time he was aware that she had moved her head a little.

Her musical voice came out of the darkness very close to him. "I can feel something a little exciting" she whispered, and there was no doubting the laughter in her voice. He felt a great sense of relief. At least he would no longer have to try and conceal his acute embarrassment. He moved his hand a little further down her back, feeling her warmth through the pyjama jacket. He longed to move his hand even further down, and explore the curve of her buttocks, but that seemed too presumptuous. Anyway, they were modestly covered by the folds of his pyjama jacket. Then she reached down, and undid the one remaining button on the front of the jacket.

"It was so very thoughtful of you to have done away with all the other buttons" she giggled, and he could not help joining in her barely suppressed laughter. He felt the warmth and softness of her breasts pressing against his chest.

"I couldn't bear sleeping with a bra on," she whispered, "much too uncomfortable."

Her left hand began to stroke his chest, and then moved down his body. He threw caution to the winds, and explored a neat, trim little bottom in similar fashion. By now something fairly large was threatening to come between them.

"You do seem to be a little excited for some reason" she chuckled. "Do I have to take precautions?"

"I've had the snip" he whispered back.

She laughed again, that lovely low musical laugh. "You really do think of everything," she said.

He kissed her then for the first time, and she responded eagerly. Her lips were very soft.

Presently, after much more exploration, she lifted her left leg a little, and guided him gently into herself. There was no sense of time then, or of hurry. Just warmth and movement, and a gradual feeling of mounting excitement, culminating in an avalanche of tumult, of moaning, and then relief, peace, and they slept.

He gradually became aware of the light in the room, the bright white light of sunshine reflected off snow, and being filtered through thin curtains. It took him some time to remember where he was and how he had come to be there.

Then, suddenly, the events of the previous evening came back to him, and he turned to look at the bed beside his head. It was empty.

On the neighbouring pillow was his orange pyjama jacket, neatly folded, and on top of that was a small piece of yellow paper torn off a memo pad. He reached a hand out from under the warmth of the bedclothes, and picked it up. His eyes took several seconds to focus.

"With my thanks to a perfect gentleman" was written on it in a very neat hand.

Perhaps she is still downstairs? He thought. He jumped out of bed and dressed very rapidly, discovering as he did so that the electricity had been restored. Down in the empty hall he picked up the bell and rang it vigorously, and after an interval the old man appeared, looking even more the worse for wear in the cold light of day.

"Is the lady still here?" he asked, rather breathlessly. The answer was terribly important to him.

The old man looked at him curiously.

"Went an hour since" he said. "I offered her what breakfast I could rustle up, but she said she must get home. She said to tell her husband to follow as soon as he could get his car going. You should be alright now, sir," he added, "the plough went through at first light, and it has not snowed since. Wind's dropped an all."

David settled up his account, picked up his bag, and went out into the shining brightness of Christmas morning.

FIVE.   THE LAST TRAIN.

Some people said that it was being christened "Wyatt" which was the cause of it all in the first place. His father, Douglas Whiteham had insisted on the name, despite his mothers rather feeble protests. His father was a great fan of the Wild West, indeed considered himself a national expert on the subject, and he held that "Wyatt" was a good, strong, masculine, no-nonsense sort of name. So Wyatt he was christened, on a damp, foggy Sunday afternoon in the month of February, in an outer suburb of Southampton. He set the tone for his future life by bawling loudly, selfishly and doggedly throughout the entire service.

Wyatt reached adolescence just in time for the "swinging sixties," the permissive society, the television culture and Doctor Beeching's axe work on the railways of Britain. By the time he slouched into his teens, Wyatt's future could be pretty accurately predicted without the aid of a fortune teller. He was set to be of moderate height, with rather a thin face, a sallow complexion, close set grey eyes, and a rather large and pointed nose, a bit like a rats. His sandy hair was invariably unkempt, and mostly unwashed, and two large and protruding ears stuck through the mop on either side. He was also a very spotty adolescent, the problem exacerbated by his generally infrequent washing habits. He smoked regularly from the age of twelve, at first surreptitiously, but after a year or two quite openly, to his father's fury, and his mothers sorrow. He also constantly chewed gum, and left the discarded gobs stuck in hiding all round the house. His poor mother was constantly finding them and trying to prise them off without his father noticing.

His clothing tended to be always tatty, with self-inflicted damage to make it trendy. The exception was a large and expensive collection of brightly coloured neck scarves, which he bought sometimes with his own money, and if that was lacking due to the cost of fags, with money "borrowed" from his mother's handbag. His mother noticed the loss of this steady trickle of money, for she kept accounts, but she was too weak and cowed to remonstrate about it.

At school Wyatt did not show any academic ability at all, nor did he demonstrate any enthusiasm or skill at any sport. But he did quickly perfect the art of bullying others. His motives appeared to be threefold, if he had been capable of analysing them, which he was not. First, he enjoyed inflicting pain on others, pure and simple. Second, bullying others made him feel big and important in the world. Third, by extracting protection money from weaker folk he could add a good deal to his income, and he needed the money as he had added drinking to his growing list of expensive hobbies. Raising money became an important object during his schooldays.

From time to time Wyatt would come across boys who were larger and stronger than himself. On such occasions he did his best to curry favour by standing them drinks, offering cigarettes, and fawning flattery. He became very good at gauging the comparison between others and himself, and acting his part accordingly. Girls he always treated as second class citizens, to be patronised, manipulated or bullied as he thought fit.

By the time Wyatts school days came to an end, he had put on three stone in weight, largely due to an excess of beer and fatty foods, and an almost total lack of exercise, and he had distinguished himself by failing to pass a single exam that was set before him. His teachers, one and all, were delighted to see the back of him, and his classmates almost arranged a celebration party on his departure, only they were too scared to do so.

Wyatt celebrated the end of his schooling by having a real binge down at his local "Saloon." He then decided to mark his passage into full adulthood by having a rest for a couple of months, and by growing an untidy beard which saved him the bother of having to shave any longer. He fondly imagined that the whiskers made him look more manly and "butch." Then, prompted by his increasingly exasperated father, he began to look around him for some sort of job which would give him the maximum financial return for the minimum of effort.

Here Wyatt encountered his first real problem in life, and it came as a great surprise to him. It seemed that for some inexplicable reason prospective employers upon whom he bestowed the privilege of a visit, did not quite share his own view of his abilities. In fact they seemed very negative about his prospects in whatever business they happened to be engaged. Wyatt very quickly ran out of likely employment opportunities.

His position further deteriorated because his father became mean and selfish when confronting his well established habits around the home, and threatened to kick him out, and his mother at length learned to keep her spare cash on her person, and not leave it in her handbag. Eventually Wyatt got a job as a builder's labourer, swapped it quite quickly at the builder's request for that of a plumber's mate, and then soon after having very nearly been brained by an irate plumber wielding a very large Stilson, he became a member of a gang who resurfaced unsuspecting peoples front drives for exorbitant sums of money. The technique followed in this profession was that the cost of the work was only disclosed after the job was said to have been completed. Wyatt, because of his size and appearance, was often chosen as the team member who went to the householder to break the news about the ultimate cost of the job, and to collect the money. This was a task which Wyatt much enjoyed actually, and especially if his victim was a woman, or elderly, or better still, both.

Wyatt actually stuck to this job, for it brought good money in, and there were a number of perks. Apart from the opportunities for harassing the weak, he was regarded with some grudging respect by his workmates for his conveniently unpleasant disposition. But further, formalities like disclosing ones true income to the Inland Revenue were entirely dispensed with. The gang moved round quite a large area of the country, of necessity, which made them very hard to trace by the authorities. By the time Wyatt was twenty four he was managing to earn a lot of money by barely legal and definitely not legal means, and he paid next to no tax. He was able to run a very flashy and fast car, and to go on exotic and alcohol fuelled holidays. In fact he spent all of his money on himself, and still sponged on his parents at home.

But for all his success, Wyatt still felt a great lack of satisfaction with his life. It was time he "settled down" he decided, and raised a family of little Wyatts.

Wyatt first saw Mary Clarke when she was serving behind the bar at the Red Lion in Emsworth. She was twenty three, between jobs, and just helping out in the pub during the holiday period. She was a shy girl, with light brown hair, a rounded face, and a pleasant complexion. She used very little make up, had kindly brown eyes and a friendly smile. Wyatt chatted her up, and made it quite clear that he was very taken with her. Mary was not quite so sure, but she accepted when Wyatt pressed her for a date on the next evening when she was free. Wyatt left the pub whistling happily. Life was being very good to him again.

Their courtship was really a very one sided affair, and afterwards in later life Mary had to admit that she should have recognised all the signs of the future so clearly displayed. Sadly, she was flattered by all the attention she received, and a little dazzled by the luxurious car and the apparently unending supply of money displayed before her. She did not even notice that most of that money remained firmly in Wyatt's back pocket. She quickly capitulated sexually in the face of Wyatts half bullying and half cajoling assault, and generally did everything he wanted her to do. Perhaps she actually wanted a masterful man. In the event she got Wyatt.

By this time Wyatt had almost got it all worked out on the back of an envelope. If he married Mary he would lose some of his independence, but not necessarily very much. Financially, she would have to get a decent job and pay her way, if she was going to pay her half share of the mortgage on a decent house. The house, of course, would be solely in Wyatts name. She would do all the cooking, and the washing of his usually filthy clothes. And he would have sex on demand whenever he felt like it. It seemed a pretty good investment for his future, even before one imagined all those wonderful little Wyatts looking up to him for guidance, and with eyes full of gratitude and respect for all he had done for them.

They were married about three months after they had first met. Mary, being rather an old fashioned girl, would have liked a quiet wedding in her local church, but Wyatt vetoed the idea immediately on the grounds of economy, and also stated that he would feel "uncomfortable" in a church, though he did not explain why.

"And if your parents have got any spare money to fling around," declared Wyatt to Mary, "it had better be put towards the deposit on our new home."

But there was to be no economy when it came to the food and especially the drink for their reception, as Wyatt wanted to make a "big splash" for all his friends.

Mary very quickly learned what was expected of her when they returned from a week of honeymoon which had given Wyatt a glorious opportunity to sate himself on the two things he liked best, drink and sex, in that order. She found that the unending supply of money largely belonged to the bank, who were beginning to look at the figures for this particular client with more care, and adjust their attitude accordingly.

Mary was required to find herself a job, or even two jobs, with all possible speed, so that Wyatt could continue to keep himself in the manner in which he wished to remain accustomed. She herself always had to exercise the most stringent economy for anything that was for herself, while he could always justify considerable expenditure on the car, drink, parties, cigarettes, and anything he decided to indulge in at that particular moment. And Mary also learnt very quickly not to question or argue if she wanted to keep her pretty face intact. Her warm smile was rarely seen, these days, and her brown eyes developed a wary look. She seemed to be always tired now, and became even more so when she became pregnant just six months into their marriage. Wyatt was delighted, and used this fact to prove his manhood to all those whom he met, as if he had done something clever that had never been done before.

It did not help, however, when Mary, after a difficult and prolonged labour, gave birth to a rather small daughter. There was no female equivalent of the name "Wyatt" that he could think of.

So several years dragged by, and in due course another child, a son, was born to them, and he was christened William, but always known as Billy the Kid by his doting father. Wyatt, now following in his father's footsteps, became more interested in the Wild West, and achieved one of his great ambitions by being permitted to join the local pistol shooting club. Many of the members did not want him, but they needed the money. Wyatt indeed spent much time and money trying to put bullets through targets which he declared he could hardly see, - mainly because he refused to wear the spectacles he needed on the grounds that they spoilt his macho image. He spent a lot of his time boring other club members, and in fact anyone he met, with exaggerated stories of his exploits and prowess at the sport.

The rest of his time, when he wasn't actually working, he continued to live a totally selfish life, which more and more revolved around his obsession with the Wild West. The arrival of the Video Recorder opened up a completely new world for him. He amassed a huge collection of Wild West films, - there seemed to be an unlimited supply, and he now spent many hours a week slouched in front of the T.V. with a can of beer in his hand. He even developed a sort of Western slang which he delighted to use on all occasions. It was a great disappointment to him that the law prohibited him from walking around with a couple of six shooters in holsters slapping against his legs!

Whilst his shooting skills might improve a little, or so he fondly believed, there was one area of Wyatt's slavish espousal of all things Wild West which continued to frustrate him, and painfully so. He could never seem to learn to ride. This was largely because he regarded a horse as simply a four legged variety of motor car. You should just be able to climb on, dig in your spurs, and sail away. Wyatt did a lot of sailing away, into some exotic and uncomfortable locations like bramble and gorse bushes, and on one very memorable occasion into a slurry pit. Words much more blistering than "tarnation" were frequently heard in the vicinity of the riding stables, and of course in every case it was entirely the fault of the horse. Miss Mackland, who ran the stables, offered Wyatt every horse in turn which she owned, and in the end was very tempted to offer her impossible cow boy a cow to try instead!

The Wild West fetish grew and grew, and life at home became almost intolerable for Mary and the children. Mary was just used as a doormat by Wyatt, whose violence towards her continued to grow, and he spent more and more time and money down at the local "saloon." By nightfall he was always drunk, and the family dreaded his return home.

Fifteen Love

It was a Friday night in mid April when Wyatt staggered in at about 11.p.m. much the worse for wear as usual. He had had a very bad day. There had been no work for the gang, so no bullying to be done and no money. He had organised a riding lesson at the last minute, and had encountered a new horse. But not for very long, for no sooner had it felt his heels being cruelly dug into its sides than it had Wyatt off in full view of half a dozen other riders and stable girls in the yard, who did not conceal their enjoyment of his rodeo performance. Sadly for his family, on these bruising occasions he never seemed to break anything significant, like his neck, for by now he was very well padded all round. This final humiliation had led to a heated exchange with Miss Mackland, who had also enjoyed his splendid exhibition, and led to her informing him that she would be most obliged if he would take his custom elsewhere. She made a mental note to ring several friends who ran riding stables in the area to warn them in advance. Wyatt was particularly angry because Miss Mackland was a forceful woman, holding a very serviceable riding crop, and he had not been able to browbeat her in at all a satisfactory manner.

After lunch at the pub, with several beers to wash away the memories of the morning, he had gone in to see his boss and collect his share of the week's takings, and found that because of the fact that he had done very little work during the week due to being "busy" elsewhere, his wages were correspondingly disappointing, in fact as he observed under his breath, hardly worth coming to collect. He was quite scared of the boss, and could do little more than whinge about it, and drag himself off with a bad grace. There would have to be economies at home, and Mary must try and get more overtime.

Wyatt adjourned to another pub to restore his self esteem by drinking hard and being rude to anyone he felt was weaker than himself. By 11.p.m. he had little money left, was drunk to the point of being quarrelsome, and he then decided to go home and "deal with Mary." Somehow he managed to convince himself that she alone was the cause of his misfortunes in life.

Wyatt banged in through the kitchen door, and very nearly fell over the dog, which was on the mat inside. He instinctively lashed out at it with his foot, but it had learned a lot through living with Wyatt for the last few years, and it dodged and scuttled under the table out of harms way. Wyatt swore at it. The he discovered on the table a note from Mary saying she had gone to bed early with a migraine, and asking him to walk the dog last thing before going to bed.

Wyatt held the note, and swore again. He suspected Mary of manufacturing these stupid headaches just to deny him his marital rights. Still, he would get even with her in the morning. As it would be a Saturday, Mary had not got to go to work. He picked up the dog lead and a stick, called to the dog, which scuttled past him, and then followed it out of the door. He lurched down the garden path at the back, through the old broken gate, and down a few steps to the disused railway line which ran along behind the row of houses. Once there, he turned right. The moon appeared fleetingly from behind a cloud, and the dog ran along in front of him, pausing to sniff the odd tuft of grass, but always keeping a safe distance from him.

Here the path ran straight and level between the banks of an old cutting, but there was nothing left to link it with the railway of the past, and the prolific bramble bushes pressed in on both sides. The dog sniffed at the recent tracks of passing rabbits. It was very still, and for some reason Wyatt suddenly felt uneasy. He decided to turn back, but his legs did not want to do so, and he found himself continuing to walk on. Eventually after five minutes, he made a great resolve to stop and turn. This he managed, and he then whistled to the dog, which was busy in a bramble patch. He called its name, his voice sounding hollow and unnatural in the silence of the night. The dog wouldn't come, so he went after it, with stick upraised, swearing a good deal.

He suddenly and unexpectedly came upon it, standing stock still in the middle of the path, and staring into the distance. The moon showed up its white fur. He cursed it, and tried to hit it with his stick. Dogs should be firmly disciplined, he had always maintained. But the dog jumped back as Wyatt swung at it, and he caught his foot in one of the many rabbit holes. He twisted round, and fell heavily on his side, across the path. His ankle throbbed with pain, and he swore even more violently.

After a couple of minutes he rolled onto his back to try and ease the pain. The dog, sensing that he was no longer a threat, came and stood beside him, but it still stared into the distance up the track. Wyatt decided that it was now time to make a great effort to get up. After all, no-one was likely to find him out here in the middle of the night. He tried to move himself, but strangely his arms and hands seemed to have lost their strength. It must be the shock of the fall, he thought. Things like that could happen, couldn't they? Then he tried to roll over, but found he could not do so. He lay still on his back, and decided to wait a minute or two and then try again.

As he lay there, a distant sound in the stillness reached his ears. It came to him as a sort of faint rustling whisper, far away. At the same time the dog beside him stiffened, and all its hair stood on end. Its lips curled, and it emitted a low, fearful growl. Wyatt felt the hair that was left on his own head stir. He tried with a great effort to roll over again, but he could not move. It was as though his arms were pinned to his sides, and his legs locked together. And then gradually he realised that there was something also behind his neck, something that felt metallic and very cold.

The distant noise, at first almost imperceptible, was a little louder, nearer. Wyatt strained his eyes upwards in the darkness. There was something up there, something gaunt, vague, towering above him. Then he started violently, as there was a rasping sound of metal moving just behind his head, and then above him a loud , hollow, echoing clang. The moon suddenly came out again, and by its eerie light Wyatt recognised the signal. He also realised, in a flash of understanding, that the noise he had heard was the signal moving. It was now in the down position, signalling for a train to come. But his mind screamed at him. There was no signal on this disused line, never had been as long as he had lived there.

Now the noise was closer, and the dog gave a final frightened growling bark, and took off up the steep bank through the bramble bushes, or at least where they had been before. They seemed to have gone. Wyatt tried to call to it, for he felt terrifying alone now.

Then, suddenly, he recognised the increasing sound. He tried desperately to move his head round, to see something, but only managed to move it an inch with great effort. The noise now had a strong note of thunder to it, and he thought he could hear the sound of a bell slowly ringing. He strained his eyes further round, craning to see further up the track. There was indeed a light there, round and white, wavering a bit, which seemed to coincide with the source of the sound, and then he felt the metal rail behind his neck begin to vibrate.

Then, with his great knowledge of the Wild West, the full horror of his situation burst in on Wyatt, and he screamed a hoarse scream of terror as with a thundering roar the train rushed upon him. And Wyatt finally lost his head.

When they eventually found his body in the morning, no one, friends, police, or coroner, could explain how Wyatt had come to be so neatly decapitated.

SIX. THE DRIVING TEST.

When a candidate comes for a driving test, we examiners do not know a lot about them in advance. This may be deliberately done to avoid any sort of preferential treatment, or even the passing of a bribe! The notes and application form revealed that my next candidate was female, eighteen years of age, that she lived in a Vicarage not so many miles from the test centre, was apparently healthy in mind and body, and had already failed the driving test three times. Her previous driving test examiners had recorded that she seemed to have an over confident trust in her own abilities when driving a car. I noted that they had all written up their reports in a rather shaky hand.

I met her in the waiting room, and asked her to conduct me to her car. It was a small, red Volkswagon, parked in the car park, and beside it stood a large, middle aged clergyman, dressed overall in a vast black cassock. He bowed to me as I approached, and his whole manner seemed extremely apprehensive. He watched with a worried expression as I made the required examination of the car, and then asked the young lady to read a number plate for me at the stipulated distance. She managed to do that very satisfactorily. I then moved towards the car, and at that moment the cleric addressed me.

"Sir, would you be so kind as to allow me to accompany my young pupil on her testing ordeal?" he asked me.

I was a little surprised, I must admit, as this is not a usual request, though quite in order. Most instructors prefer not to see the result of their tuition at close quarters.

"You are indeed the ladies driving instructor?" I asked.

"Yes, verily" he replied, "We have laboured together in the vineyard in the heat of the day. She is also the child of my loins."

I could think of no suitable reply to that one, and as I wondered how many vineyards exactly they had driven

81

through, having a vision of miles of uprooted vines, I gave my permission for him to accompany us. The large clergyman pushed the front seat forward, and slowly eased his wobbling bulk into the back, where he seemed to occupy it totally. His daughter meanwhile hopped nimbly into the driving seat, and I pulled the front seat back and climbed into the passenger seat.

I turned to the vast clergyman behind me.

"You must remember," I said "that at no time during the test run should you communicate with the driver or myself."

"No, no," replied our back seat passenger, "to be sure, no, never!"

I then requested my candidate to start up the car, drive out of the car park and turn to the right.

"Oh Lord," said a voice from the back, which I did not immediately recognise because of its strange parsonical quality, "be with us, we pray we, on this our coming journey, that we may go upon our business in safety all the days of our life, Amen."

I looked round quickly, but our reverend friend was sitting quietly, his head bowed and his eyes closed. We started off with a definite jerk, and I turned quickly back to view the scene in front.

After about three hundred yards we came to the High Street, and I requested that we should turn left. It was a busy morning, and as we proceeded at a smart pace, the voice from the back was heard once again, "O Gracious Lord" it prayed, "we beseech thee to keep in the safety the elderly couple crossing the road there in front of us, for in truth they are on a pedestrian crossing."

Our driver slowed slightly, and the elderly couple were indeed preserved, making it safely to the pavement a full second before we passed them. I glanced round at our intercessor, but his eyes appeared to be tight shut, and his posture suggested nothing but reverend meditation.

Fifteen Love

We turned right at the traffic lights at the end of the High Street, without incident, passed the shopping centre and the council offices, and approached the large roundabout.

"O Omnipotent Lord," suddenly intoned the voice from the rear seat again, "we thank Thee that Thou hast ordained in Thy goodness that we should give way at roundabouts to traffic from the right, for so it hath seemed good unto Thee."

I turned fully round, and gave the back seat a hard stare, but I was again apparently unseen for our passenger's eyes remained tightly closed. My candidate duly slowed up, and gave way at the roundabout, but it seemed to me that there might be a hint of mutiny in her bearing now.

I then asked her to pull into the kerb and park, which she managed very well. Then I instructed her to reverse back and into the side turning just behind us. As she turned round to look through the back window for this manoeuvre, her clerical father threw himself across the back seat in a vast still wobbling mass as he tried to get below her line of sight. He only partially succeeded due to excess bulk. His daughter then reversed round the corner at some speed, and to crown her effort rather light heartedly mounted the kerb, before applying the handbrake and stalling the engine.

"O Lord," prayed a very muffled voice, "thou knowest all our faults, and art most ready to forgive and forget….."

"Now" I said very firmly, putting an immediate stop to further orations from the rear, "we shall pull out onto the main road, turning left, and once we are moving, and if the road behind is clear, I shall bang with this file on the dashboard, and I want you to do a controlled emergency stop. Is that quite clear?"

"Yes" answered our driver, and we set off, turning left onto the larger road.

"Stop!" I said firmly, banging on the dashboard, after we had gone about a quarter of a mile. My candidate stood on her brakes fiercely, and a huge heavy soft object cannoned into the back of our seats.

"God…" said a breathless voice. It was the shortest prayer of the entire journey.

We started off once again, and continued down to the ring road, which was very busy with continuous traffic, and I instructed that we should turn right, which is one of the most difficult challenges of the whole test. As we waited, not very patiently, the voice gave tongue again,   " Lord, Thou didst hold back the Red Sea to let Moses and his host cross in safety, hold back, we pray, this tide of cars that we may proceed in due season upon our lawful occasions."

I looked to the left, expecting to see a sudden pile up of oncoming cars, but instead there was a reasonable gap into which we shot with a considerable jerk. I made a note on my pad, and wondered whether I should say anything. It was a bit tricky, however, as my Manual of Instructions said nothing about the offering of prayers that I could recollect.

We proceeded down the wide ring road, busy with hurrying traffic, where many a candidate has exceeded the forty miles an hour speed limit unwittingly in the past, simply by keeping up with the speeding traffic in front. It was a favourite trap of mine, and I was just about to tap the speedometer, and make a note on my board, when the voice of prayer was heard again:

" O Lord, whose servant Jehu didst drive so furiously, remind us that in this our day we are subject to speed limits upon our roads, as truly signified by that round sign which we may perceive if we are truly alert. Amen."

I turned right round in my seat to confront the Old Testament scholar this time, for he had definitely gone too far, and at the same time his daughter slowed down sufficiently to avoid my strictures. Her father's face had an expression of smug reverence, with no trace of a smile however. Thwarted, I turned round and resumed my job.

" I would like you to turn left at the next turning, "I instructed my candidate, "and then stop on the hill in front of you. We shall then do a hill start."

We duly turned left, and approached the hill, and as we did so I could palpably feel the tension rising on the back seat. We stopped at the correct place and the handbrake was efficiently applied.

"Please start and proceed up the hill when you are ready" I said to the candidate. She took a deep breath and reached for the handbrake, but in fact it was her father who started first:

"Gracious Lord, Thou knowest our present situation, give us we beseech thee a happy issue out of all our afflictions….."

His final words were drowned by the rising crescendo of the engine, and he was pinned back in his seat, as I was, when the car suddenly shot forward in an apparent effort to shake itself free of the earth's gravity and go into orbit. We charged over the top of the hill, and I gave rather breathless instructions about the next turning. This was negotiated safely, without any further prayer, and we drove through a residential area at a modest speed. At the end of one road I indicated that we should turn left at the next T Junction. There was a clear "Stop" sign at this point, but our clerical passenger was too shaken up to notice it. My candidate, possibly placing too much reliance on father in the back, did not notice it either. We skipped out onto the new road, clipping the kerb as we did so. There was a heavy bump at the rear, followed by a sharp intake of breath on the back seat as our passenger suddenly realised what his protégé had just done. I made a clear note on my pad, and as I did so a new and more urgent prayer began:

"Merciful Lord" intoned the voice, very unctuously, "you know the sins of us all, and art most ready to forget and forgive; soften, we pray thee, the heart of this good man that he too may overlook our many faults, and be pleased to forgive and forget, that we may continue in peace and happiness all the days of our lives."

I glanced down at my board to see all the faults I was expected to forgive and forget, then I am afraid hardened my heart and did not alter the comments on the pad, instead giving my next directions:

"Through the traffic lights at the appropriate time, and then right onto the ring road again, please." The lights changed to amber just as we approached them, and for a moment I thought my candidate was going to jump them, for she had the expression of a rider on a very spirited horse approaching a high fence. However, at the last moment she braked hard, and her father in the back again collided with the front seats. They were complicated traffic lights, with separate green arrows for turning left or right. Our driver had obviously considered that we had waited long enough in anybody's book, and as soon as the first arrow, indicating a left turn, lit up, she charged out at speed and turned right. Fortunately she just missed the car which was turning into our road from the right, but it was a narrow thing, and provoked a blast on the other driver's horn, and a nervous squeak from the rear seat. I made yet another note, and waited with interest for the inevitable prayer from behind. But for once our faithful pastor was bereft of words, probably also having intercepted a forceful gesture from the driver of the car we had so nearly hit.

We drove down the ring road again at a good speed, and I noticed a milk float in front of us, bumbling slowly back to the depot having finished the days deliveries, and with its batteries feeling now very weak. My driver at that moment saw it too, and it aroused all her competitive instincts, for she had not so far been able to overtake anything else, and the frustration was beginning to mount up. She pulled out into the outside lane of the dual carriageway without looking in her mirror, or giving a signal, straight into the path of a fast moving BMW. As the

driver also peeled his horn, and stood on his brakes, our resident cleric began in a nervous squeak,
" O Lord, thou knowest all….."
Our driver swerved wildly to her left, staring now into her driving mirror, her mouth open, and collided into the side of the milk float. As a flock of full and empty milk bottles hurtled round us, the prayer ended abruptly with the one word
"Help!"

SEVEN. BONI M'BUNGA'S BEES.

If you look in the learned Journals and Encyclopaedias, you will discover that Sir Alexander Flemming is credited with the discovery of Penicillin, that wonder drug of our modern world. But the learned scholars of our world do not always know it all, and I, for one, feel that equal credit should go to Boni M'Bunga and his friends.

In June of the year 1936, my father, Captain Oliver Tyler, was recently returned from fifteen years working as a soldier settler in East Africa, and he had occasion to pay a visit to a specialist in Harley Street while in London, for he suspected he was subject to mild recurring bouts of malaria. In those far off days specialists had more time for their patients, and this man was particularly interested to hear about my fathers experiences in Kenya. In due course they got onto the subject of wounds and healing, a great interest of the specialist, and my father told him one of his favourite stories, about the adventure of Boni M'Bunga.

One day in October 1931, while living at Molo in Kenya, my father had discovered that his larder was rather more empty than he thought, so spurred on by his wife, he decided to organise a hunting trip as soon as possible to remedy the situation. Accordingly, two days later, on a bright crisp morning, they set out from the timber yard in the by now rather aged Chevrolet truck, and bounced off down the road to the North East, heading for the lower slopes of Mount Kenya, about fifty miles away. This was an area noted for abundant game, and it was my fathers hope that they would at least find plenty of buck there, and even perhaps an Eland if they were lucky. What else they might come across would be anybody's guess, and at times the hunters could easily become the hunted! My father drove the truck, with his chief hunter sitting beside him, cradling his hunting rifle. A dozen other men stood up in the back of the truck, laughing and chattering, clutching their spears and keeping their balance in the bouncing swaying truck with effortless ease. Most of them were members of the Masai tribe, famed for their hunting ability, and among their number was Boni M'Bunga. Boni was overjoyed to be included on a trip which promised a pleasant break from work for several days, - work involved cutting down trees, dragging them to the sawmill and then cutting them up, but it would also be a break from domestic life, and the noisy and continuous demands of two small children and a large wife, together with other more distant relations. Not only would he be paid extra money for the trip, but there might well be some meat to be shared out at the end of it, which would please his wife. Every way you looked at it, it was a winner, and Boni had a huge grin on his face as they bumped along the track.

When they came to the settlement at Elburgon, they turned east, on the "main" road to Nakuru and Nairobi. Here the going was better, and they travelled all through the heat of the day, leaving a long dust cloud behind them. They stopped briefly in the little town of Nakuru to buy a few extra supplies, including ammunition, and then pressed on to the east, pausing only twice to mend the inevitable punctures.

When they reached the right track, they swung left off the road, and Mount Kenya lay before them in the distance, its peak swathed in cloud. Now the track was pretty rough, and they had to ford three rivers, having a considerable job pulling the truck through one of them. Finally, just before dusk, they came literally to the end of the road, and under some trees nearby they set up a camp site, and erected their tents. The cook and an assistant would be left there to guard the truck and look after home base for the expedition.

Early next morning, soon after dawn, my father led his hunting party out of camp, and they headed up into the foothills of the mountain. They had a reasonable amount of success on this first day, largely due to the tracking expertise of the hunters, but it was mid afternoon when three of the party were skinning a Duika that my father noticed Boni M'Bunga's scar. Boni had shed most of his scanty clothing for this messy operation, and as he bent over the dead animal he revealed a large scar on his lower back.

"Who gave you that hurt then, Boni?" my father asked.

Boni stood up and faced my father, with a big grin on his face. He pointed to his stomach, where there was another large scar, about six or seven inches long. He then turned back to the job in hand, and my father was distracted by another hunter who had found some promising recent footprints nearby which indicated a large buck in the neighbourhood.

When dusk came, they had added another buck to the bag, and they found a level space among some bushes and prepared to make camp for the night. Some of the small thorn trees were cut down to provide firewood, and create a low barricade to keep out prowling animals. Meat was prepared for roasting over the fire, and each man selected and prepared a sleeping place. At that altitude nights were surprisingly cold, so the fire was kept burning all night, both to keep them a little warmer, and for protection. Even lions will keep away from a fire, but my father always slept with his loaded rifle beside him as an extra precaution.

After a good supper, they sat round the fire and talked, and the conversation inevitably developed into favourite hunting stories, some of which my father had heard several times before! As he looked across the circle of squatting figure, lit up by the firelight, my father again spotted Boni and remembered the scars on his body.

"Now Boni," said my father, when there was a pause in the stories, "you tell me about those two scars you have there on your body."

Boni proved reluctant at first, but when he was encouraged by the others, and had taken another drink from a cup of local wine, which the Masai brew with great skill, he began his story, slowly at first, but then with increasing animation.

Some four years before, Boni and about a dozen young men from his village had decided to go on a special hunting trip. They told their families that they were just going to find meat, and were thus commended for their efforts. In fact, they were after a much more exotic and valuable prize. The aphrodisiac properties of rhino horn may not stand up to thorough scientific investigation, but East Africa was not the only part of the world where many men and women pinned their hopes on its efficacy. Boni and his young friends were after rhino, which is a very dangerous occupation as a rhino has very different and determined ideas as to what his horn is best used for!

For the first two days they had no luck, finding only small buck. The only rhino traces they saw were very old. But on the third day they found fresh tracks by a water hole, made that very morning. Moreover, they were very large deep tracks in the soft ground, indicating a very large animal, with probably a very substantial ration of horn. There was much excitement and anticipation as they swiftly followed the clear tracks through the grass for an hour or so, and then came at length to an area of small scrub thorn trees. The trees were surrounded on three sides by low scree cliffs. By now it was getting towards noon, the heat of the day, and they were pretty sure the rhino had gone in among the trees to rest until it got cooler. Two of the hunters crept round the grove of trees, and confirmed that there were no tracks leading out the other side.

A whispered debate then followed. No one very much liked the idea of going in after the rhino, so it was decided to flush him out. The hunters took up positions round the thicket, and a fire was kindled up-wind. Some of the thorn bushes caught fire, but it seemed ages before a sudden crashing in the undergrowth indicated that their quarry was on the move. In the event, he moved a lot faster than they had anticipated, charging through a gap between two hunters, neither of whom scored a hit with their spears, and galloping off across the grassland, at a very good speed. The whole hunting party followed at top speed, giving tongue as much as lack of breath permitted. The rhino had got a good start, and maintained his good lead for a couple of miles, but at length he made a strange and costly mistake. They came to an area of broken ground, with boulders, small craggy ridges and gullies. The rhino, by now tiring a good deal, charged into the entrance of one of these gullies, and found itself in a cul-de-sac. However, it was still full of fight, and very angry as well, and it quickly turned and prepared to fight its way back out of it. Boni was up with the leaders, and they quickly took station up the sides of the gully, and prepared to confront their adversary. As they advanced slowly towards it, the cornered rhino waved its huge horn about threateningly. At length one of the hunters threw his spear, and grazed the animal's side, whereupon it put its head down and charged back down the gully. Boni and the others raised their spears, but it was at that moment that Boni's foot slipped on a damp mossy rock. He had a fearful memory of cart wheeling through the air, and then a great pain in his lower body, and then merciful oblivion.

  Boni fell silent at this point, but another hunter round the fire who had been present on that fateful occasion took up the tale. He described how he saw Boni fall from the rock into the path of the charging rhino. The next moment he saw Boni impaled on the rhino's horn, and lying across its nose as it ran down the gully. The sudden arrival of Boni must have been pretty surprising for the rhino as well, particularly as his inert body now blinded it. It ran on for twenty yards, and then stumbled over a rock, as it could no longer see where it was going. The resulting jerk was nearly fatal for Boni, but the delay enabled his friends to close in and this time several spears found their mark. After a bloody tousle, the rhino was dispatched, and Boni's friends lifted his limp body off the great horn, and laid it on the grass beneath the shade of a scrub thorn tree.

After a few minutes of contemplation and sorrowful self reproach, with a bit of superstition thrown in for good measure, the party began to look for a good place to dig a shallow grave in the rocky ground. They found a spot at length, some distance away, and after careful inspection returned for the body. Fortunately, just at the moment that the burial party arrived, Boni had stirred and groaned. A rhino horn, for all its savage appearance, is actually a very smooth and well polished object, and the horn had done amazingly little damage to the hunter in its passage right through him.

His friends at once sprang into action. There was a special procedure for first aid well known to them all. They would need a special type of grass, and a thorn needle for stitching, and a bee's nest. No problem with the former, but the bees might not be too keen on co-operating. One of the hunters knew of a bee's nest not too far away in a small cliff, so a group of the hunters was sent off to fetch it.

The nest was about twelve feet up, in a hole, and a difficult climb. The group picked out the youngest and most athletic member of their company, and despite his protests about his lack of experience and fitness, they clothed him in almost every garment they possessed, and then stood well back as he slowly ascended the cliff. The bees seemed to know what he was about, and fired a few warning stings. When he got to the hole, he was able to break the sides away with his spear, and then scoop the whole nest out. He arrived back on the ground quite close to the nest, having gathered a few more stings, and then legged it into a nearby bush. After a few minutes, when the bees had settled on the nest and were inspecting their new situation, he crept out and threw a cotton cloth over the whole nest.

His friends now gathered round, and they quickly kindled a fire a few feet from the nest and to windward. When it was blazing nicely, they put handfuls of grass on it, and then lifted the edge of the piece of cloth, so that the bees got well and truly smoked. In ten minutes the inhabitants of the nest were either fully overcome, or had pushed off to start again elsewhere. The party wrapped the nest in the piece of cloth, (it was somebody's loin cloth, actually) and returned triumphant if a little stung, to Boni and his medical team.

They were very pleased to find Boni was still alive, as that made it all seem worthwhile. They had discussed on the way back what to do if Boni had departed this life, and they were unanimous that it was in order to eat the honey themselves!

Carefully, they set to work, starting on Boni's front. The wound was plugged with a mixture of honey, wax, and dead smoked bees. Then the skin was carefully stitched up with the grass, and when everyone was agreed that it was a good job, - Boni's opinion was not asked as he did not feel too good, then they gently attended to his back, repeating the procedure as before. By this time Boni was only semi conscious, and not really aware of the well meant medical attention he was receiving.

Not too far away there was a small grove of trees, and a fairly large boulder. They tenderly carried Boni over to it, and sat him up against the boulder. He would be in the shade there. Then they set about making him a fire. This was kindled a few feet away from him, and a lot of firewood was collected and put in a pile within his reach. Boni was by now fully conscious again, but he just sat and watched. Soon they placed his spear beside him, leaning against the boulder, by his right hand, and then they placed a small parcel of meat wrapped in leaves, and a gourd with water in it by his left hand. Boni did not question what they did or why, for he knew perfectly well. Nor was he surprised when after about an hour each member of the band came over to him, and took formal leave of him, and then the group moved off, carrying the precious rhino horn between them. They were leaving him to "do or die" as was their custom, and Boni knew that according to their religious beliefs they would never take back to the village a man who was likely to die. If he did so, then that would bring bad luck on the whole community.

My father had some difficulty in persuading Boni to describe the next few days in his life. He was uncertain how long he sat propped against the boulder, but his friends reckoned it was three days. As it got dark, the fire was his source of comfort, as well as of warmth and security. His ears strained to hear the noises he dreaded in the African night, like snortings, howlings, the rustle of something in the grass, and twigs being snapped. At times he caught a glimpse of a dark shape just beyond the firelight, and twice eyes gleamed and glared at him. He clutched his spear in terror, and did not dare sleep. Once an animal approached closer to the fire, and he heard it growl. He shook his spear at it, but did not dare throw it, knowing that if he did he would lose his only means of defence. Once he heard a sound behind the boulder against which he sat, and in terror he hurled his empty water gourd backwards over his head.

By day it was very hot, but he had to keep his precious fire alight. His scanty meat was soon eaten, and his water exhausted. No one from the village came out to see him. The second night was worse than the first, for he sensed that there were animals lurking nearby, just waiting for him to die. They were probably hyenas, the best scavengers in the bush. Somehow he got through, but he realised now that if he did not go in search of food and water, he risked dying of starvation and thirst, if not from his wounds. Slowly, and with the aid of his spear, he pulled himself to his feet, and leaned dizzily against the boulder. But his strength returned a little, and he staggered through the trees, and began the long walk back to his village, guided by his hunter's instinct for direction.

The third night was the most frightening of all, for Boni had no fire to protect him. He tried to climb a tree, but he was too weak to manage it. All he could do was clamber onto a low branch, and lie along it, clutching his spear. Sleep was impossible, but slowly the night passed, and dawn found him on the move once again. He came to a wonderful water hole, and slaked his thirst. Some animals waited for him to drink, before taking their turn. So, as the dusk came, Boni at last came to his home.

He received a rather mixed reception, actually. First, they all thought he was a ghost, and after shrieks of panic he had the village to himself for several minutes, while everyone hid in terror. Then, when he had convinced them he was truly alive, they besought him to go away in case he should die and bring them bad luck. Finally, a big girl of forceful personality who had smiled at Boni quite often in the past, marched up to him, as he sat exhausted on a log, and brought him food and drink. Boni ate ravenously, and again slaked his thirst, inwardly vowing that he would never forget the girl's courage or her kindness.

From then on Boni made a rapid and complete recovery, nursed by the girl, who in a short space of time became Mrs Boni M'Bunga. Boni became something of a local celebrity, and for a time he was often asked to demonstrate his scars and tell the story of how he acquired them, - a story which sometimes got somewhat embroidered in the telling.

The Harley Street specialist looked very thoughtful.
"That is a very interesting and remarkable story, Captain Tyler," he said.

"Perhaps you can give me a clue to one thing that has always puzzled me" replied my father. "Those Masai hunters stuffed Boni's deep wounds with a ghastly mixture of honey, beeswax and bees scooped out of a rock. I should have expected the poor man to develop a massive infection and die within days in agony."

"Ah" said the specialist, "that is what makes your story so interesting to me. I have recently been working with others to develop this amazing new substance called penicillin. It is the most miraculous cure for infection in wounds that we have ever known. And just now we have discovered that of all the substances we know, honey contains the highest percentage of pure penicillin. There could have been no better remedy than honey to treat the poor mans wounds, and his friends were well aware of it."

Which is why I seriously feel that Boni M'Bunga deserves a place in the medical Hall of Fame, as a joint discoverer, with his friends and forbears, of penicillin!

EIGHT. THE MURDERING RING.

The thief worked quickly that Christmas night, as all thieves have to do. Within half a minute of forcing the bedroom window of the elderly widow's bungalow, and having checked that his informant was correct when he said she was away with her family over Christmas, he was ransacking the top drawers of the old fashioned chest of drawers in her bedroom. His nimble fingers flipped open an old faded brown box, extracted the much worn Engagement Ring from within, and discarded the box onto the floor. The ring was transferred to his left hand, which already held two brooches, and all three were then slipped into his pocket. Other items, a watch, a well worn string of pearls, and some war medals joined them. His torch probed into the bottom of the drawer, but there was nothing else. The other drawer contained nothing but scarves, handkerchiefs and stockings. All very disappointing. He left them scattered on the floor.

Then his accomplice came hurrying from the other end of the house.

"We've struck treasure, Jonnie Boy!" he said. "I've found a bloomin' safe. Reckon we can lift it together with a bit of luck."

Jonnie ran after him. They could indeed lift it, with a struggle, and they got it back to the bedroom window, through which they had forced their entry. They nearly ruptured themselves getting it up and through the window, and they did not do the window frame a lot of good in the process, but speed was now essential. They laboured down the garden path, one in front of the other, and through the small gate into the twitten. From there it was a slow and painful trip the hundred yards to where they had left their car. The safe fitted easily into the boot, for though it was very heavy it was not large.

Five minutes later they ran the car into a lock up garage that Jonnie rented, and closed the door behind them, so that it was safe to turn on the light. They off loaded the safe onto the floor with great difficulty, and then had a stiff drink of whisky from a bottle kept up on a shelf. Jonnie then examined the safe, turning it over to look underneath. He tried a large screwdriver round the lid, but that was very secure.

"Looks like the bottom is our best bet" he muttered. "It seems to have been riveted on, and it's pretty old and rusty. Pass me the jemmy and that hammer."

Together they set to work, trying not to make too much noise, even though the nearest house was some distance away. No-one would be awake now on Christmas night. Speed was still essential as this was always a crucial part of the operation.

It took them ten minutes of swearing and sweating to get the bottom partly off. A stream of sawdust rewarded their efforts, which they scattered all over the floor.

"Someone will have to clear up all this bloomin mess" said Jonnie.

When the sawdust was all out, it revealed a second metal skin. Jonnie threw caution to the winds, and used the hammer and a cold chisel. The metal skin was not very thick, and gave way fairly easily. Now at last they could pull out the contents.

There were letters, old insurance policies, receipts, an out of date passport, some share certificates, a small quantity of foreign currency, more old letters, and a small dark red cardboard box. Their faces fell and their language ripened as they looked through their haul with mounting disappointment. Jonnie opened the small red box. Within it was a large, heavy, dull gold coloured ring, set with a single red stone. It was a type of mans signet ring, only heavier. Jonnie gave the red stone a quick polish, but even he could see at once it was not a ruby. Semi-precious only, worse luck. He slipped the ring into his pocket, along with the other things.

They kept the share certificates, the passport and the foreign money, and stuffed all the rest of the stuff through the hole into the safe again. Then they loaded the safe into the boot, did a perfunctory tidy up of the garage, had another good swig of whisky, for, as Jonnie said, it was now Christmas Day, and then opened the garage door and drove quietly out. When they were half a mile outside the village boundary, they stopped the car in a small lay-by, which had good visibility up and down the deserted road. Jonnie got the spare wheel out first, and propped it against the car in a prominent position, to provide an excuse if anyone should stop to see what was going on. Then having carefully checked to see that nothing was coming up or down the road, they manhandled the safe out of the boot and through the gate into the field beside the road. They dumped it in the ditch, and did not even attempt to cover it up with anything. Jonnie thought of giving it a parting kick, but decided he would only hurt his foot.

"Bloomin thing," he muttered, "much more trouble than it was worth."

Once back in the car Jonnie lit a cigarette, and took a deep breath.

"I always feel a lot better when I've got rid of the body" he observed.

"Wish we'd got a bit more to show for it all" replied his companion.

"Those share things may be worth a packet" said Jonnie. "Cheer up, its Christmas night, and we'll go up to Horsham to see Gary at once."

It was a quick trip with no traffic, but Jonnie drove carefully, keeping to speed limits. The police might well be out, and the last thing one wanted was to be stopped by a copper, and asked awkward questions. Gary lived in a very nice detached house up a short drive, and suitably private. It had a very prosperous look about it, a fact not lost on his visitors. They rang the door bell a couple of times, and after several minutes of waiting, Gary opened the door to them, dressed in a very expensive looking silk dressing gown. He did not look in the least surprised to find he had two visitors at 3.a.m. on Christmas morning, and led them without ceremony into his study. He switched on a powerful table lamp on his desk, bade them sit down on two chairs in front of him, and produced a tray with three glasses on it and another bottle of rather better quality whisky.

Jonnie emptied out the contents of his pocket onto the desk, and his companion added the contents of the carrier bag he was holding. Gary began to look through the things without further comment, while the other two looked on somewhat apprehensively, and drank their whisky. The small amount of jewellery he put on one pile, the medals, buttons and oddments on another, and the foreign currency on a third. He then sorted through the papers, putting the passport to one side.

"These share certificates are of no value" he observed.

Jonnie and his companion both looked crestfallen.

"But it says on them they are worth thousands" said Jonnie, in disbelief.

"Only if you can prove that you are the owner of the shares" explained Gary. "You try and pass one of those, Jonnie lad, and you'll have the cops standing on your doorstep in minutes."

Jonnie looked very glum, and his companion stuffed the certificates very hastily back in the carrier bag.

"Very little here" said Gary at length, after he had scrutinised the items of jewellery under his desk lamp. "I can give you two hundred for the lot."

"Must be worth more than that" pleaded Jonnie, but he knew he was on a loser.

"Sorry" said Gary, standing up. "Two hundred, take it or leave it. And quickly please, as I've got a nice warm bed waiting for me upstairs."

Jonnie looked at his companion, who nodded reluctantly. Gary went to a wall safe, hidden behind a picture of the South Downs, and took out a wad of notes. He counted out ten twenty pound notes, and handed them to Jonnie. The size of the wad was not apparently diminished at all. "I shall know which house to visit next time I do a job" thought Jonnie to himself.

A few minutes later they left, and the car swung out of the drive and away. Jonnie's companion sat clutching the carrier bag.

"What shall we do with this worthless rubbish?" he asked.

At that moment Jonnie noticed a skip in the road in front of them, next to a building site. He braked sharply and stopped beside it.

"Chuck the whole bag in there," said Jonnie, "but make sure no-one sees you at it."

They both checked the road to make sure it was clear, and then the bag was tossed into the skip, to be found a few days later.

"Its going to be a rotten Christmas on this lot, "muttered Jonnie's companion, "I was banking on this for everything."

Jonnie was too angry to make any response, for it exactly summed up his own position.

It was 5.a.m. when Jonnie, fortified with more whisky, and not much richer, crawled into bed, waking up his wife in the process.

"Where the hell have you been since closing time?" she demanded.

"Out with Father Christmas" replied Jonnie grimly, "now belt up or you know what you will get!"

Memories of previous black eyes and worse convinced his wife on the spot that it would be unhealthy to ask Jonnie any more questions. She had a pretty good idea how he got the money to run a large powerful car, drink like a fish, and gamble on the horses. But there was never any spare money when "luxuries" like food and clothing were needed by the family!

Understandably, Jonnie was very tired on Christmas Day. He kept going until the afternoon, with a bad grace and a very bad temper, and then went to sleep in front of the television, having threatened to disembowel the kids if they made any noise that disturbed him.

He had a vivid dream

He was walking through a cloister, on a sultry, heavy day, led on by the sound of chanting music. He came to a small door at the end of the archways, and passing through it he found himself climbing a spiral stone staircase. It all seemed very old and worn. It was a long way up, and as he climbed the chanting seemed louder and nearer. At the top he came out on a ledge with a low parapet. He looked down, and what he saw scared him stiff. Below him was the choir of the great Abbey Church, lit by the faint light coming through the stained glass windows, and also by a hundred candles in sconces on the walls, and in candelabra round about the High Altar. Several hundred monks were singing the office of Evensong, the music of the Plainsong chant echoing away among the great pillars into the distant shadows.

Suddenly, Jonnie was aware of another noise, from outside. The clank and clash of metal, upraised voices, some shouting and a scream. The singing in the Abbey wavered, but then resumed. The monks no longer sang with bowed heads, but looked apprehensively down the long nave to the west door. In a moment the doors crashed open, and a band of armed men spilled into the church, their swords gleaming in the candlelight. The singing came to a ragged stop. The soldiers advanced down the nave. From his seat near the Altar the Abbot rose, and moved out into the centre of the choir, facing the oncoming men.

"I will deal with these intruders" he cried in a ringing voice, "brothers, go quickly now in peace."

The monks made speedily for the two doors leading out on either side of the choir. Even so, some were caught and manhandled by the advancing soldiery. The Abbot stood his ground, on the top step in front of the Altar. A solder in golden armour advanced towards him, and stood arrogantly, legs apart, sword in hand.

"Abbot John" he cried, "we come with a commission from King Henry to dissolve this monastery. You have so far refused to co-operate with the Kings officers, legally sent to you. This then is your last chance."

The Abbot stood still, looking calmly down on the scene, and the now empty Abbey. The soldier below him turned to the men closest to him. "Seize me this man" he ordered.

Four soldiers advanced on the Abbot, their swords in their hands. The Abbot continued to stand still. One soldier grabbed at his hand, and the Abbot with a quick movement thrust him away. Another man seized his arm. The first soldier again grabbed his hand, and saw upon the Abbots finger his great gold ring. With a savage movement he tried to pull it off, but the Abbot was too quick for him, and curled his fingers into a fist. With a curse, the soldier raised his sword and slashed at the Abbots wrist. The tendons were severed, and the Abbots hand fell, slackly open. The man seized the ring and pulled it off.

Slowly the Abbot raised his other arm, restrained through he was, and uttered loud words in a language Jonnie could not understand. But he felt the meaning of the curse penetrate his very being, and he shivered with fear. Then the soldiers fell upon the Abbot, and murdered him on the steps of the Altar.

As the Abbot died, the candles guttered and went out one by one, and then a terrible darkness prevailed. Jonnie tried desperately to wake himself up, but he could not do so. Instead, he felt as though he had pitched forward over the parapet, and was falling. Terror overwhelmed him, but he did not strike the stone floor, and gradually he became aware that he was in a room. It was a small, sparsely furnished bedroom, and there was an old woman propped up in the old fashioned bed. He could make out her white gown and cap by the light of the single candle.

The door opened, and a tall man entered the room, stooping a little. He was dressed in a smart uniform, with a blue coat and white breeches. He carried a black cocked hat in his hand.

"Come to say goodbye, Henry?" said the old woman.

"I'm afraid so" replied her son, "I do so much wish I should not have to leave you, and especially when I know you are not well. But as you know my ship must sail on this afternoons tide."

"I quite understand, dear," said the old woman, looking him up and down. "How proud your dear father would have been to see you in your uniform. Never in his wildest dreams did he imagine that one day you would be captain of your own ship, and an East Indiaman too."

"Only a very small one" said her son, with a laugh.

"Well, you take great care of her," said the old lady, "and don't get your feet wet. Now I've something to give you. Where did I put my purse?"

She fished about under the pillows and produced a black purse, very worn, while her son watched her with interest. From it she extracted a small piece of velvet, done up in a ribbon. She untied it, and revealed a heavy gold ring with a large red stone set in it.

"You are please to take this" she said. "It was your dear father's, and he said it must always be kept in the family. He took great care of it all his life."

The captain took the gold ring from his mother, and looked closely at it. It was indeed a man's heavy signet ring, with an ornate pattern engraved in the gold. And the large, dull red stone.

Jonnie recognised the ring at once. It was the one they had found in the safe, the one they had seized from the dying Abbot. It all seemed hazy, and rather menacing.

"I will take great care of it, mother," said the man. He tried the ring on his finger, but it was really too large. He slipped it into his pocket.

"Now I must very sadly leave you" he said. "It should not be a long voyage at this time of the year, and I shall bring you back a special gift from the West Indies." He went over to the bed and kissed his mother, and then turned and left the room, raising one hand in a salute.

Jonnie was left watching the old lady in her bed. She tried to sleep, but was restless. Time passed. Suddenly there was a creaking sound on the stairs outside her room. The old lady, who had been dozing, woke up and called out "Is that you, Emily?"

Two men pushed open the door and came into the room. Both were unshaven, and with unkempt hair, and dressed in tatty clothing. One carried a wooden baton, about two feet long. The old lady shrank down in the bed, and screamed.

"Shut up, you" said one of the men roughly. "Fix her, Sam."
Sam went over to the bed, dragged one of the pillows from under the old lady's head, and smothered her face with it. She struggled, but she was weak, and he bore down with all his weight. After a few minutes the old lady ceased to move any more, and Sam slowly lifted the pillow and peered at her purple and puffed up face. Meanwhile his companion was ransacking the room in a way that Jonnie easily recognised. Sam turned and grinned, an evil, partly toothless grin, and then the room gradually got darker, but still Jonnie could not wake up, and Sam's evil grin did not fade.

Then he found he was looking in through a small round window. The cramped room inside had wood paneled walls, and was lit by a lamp which hung from a hook in the wooden ceiling. After a few moments, Jonnie realised he was looking into the cabin of a ship. There was a table in the middle of the floor, and two men sat at it, opposite one another. One of the men Jonnie at once recognised as the sea captain whose mother had been murdered. There was a bottle and two glasses on the table, and another bottle on the floor of the cabin. The two men were playing cards, saying very little but playing tensely and earnestly.

A new hand was dealt. The captain, facing Jonnie, quickly sorted his cards, discarded some, and took the same number of cards from a small pile on the table. The other man did the same, following him.

The captain said "A point of five."

"Not good. I have six in hearts," replied the younger man.

"The devil you have," said the captain, "Then my carte is no good either?"

"No" said his opponent, "I have a quinte."

"Three kings?" asked the captain, without much hope.

"Fourteen queens" said the young man, with a trace of smugness.

"Devil take it" replied the captain, and took a long drink from his glass. "You start with ninety five points, and it's the last hand, and it's supposed to be my senior. I hardly know what to lead."

He tossed an Ace onto the table. It took the trick, and he followed it with the King. Another Ace followed, and then he paused. Finally he tossed the Knave of Spades onto the pile, saying "four." The young man took it with the Queen, and then proceeded to lead the Ace of Hearts. The captain, with a sigh, put the unprotected King onto it. The young man looked a little smug again as he led out his remaining five Hearts, and his last

Queen, which took the last trick. The hand had come to a swift end, and the captain was counting up his score. He made a note on a piece of card.

"Four tricks and a lead," he muttered. "Five. That makes a total of eighty eight for the game. You've rubiconed me again. Good and proper." He took another long drink from his glass, and sat staring at it. The younger man gathered up the cards.

"I shall have to stop there, Charles Hannington" he said, "can't remember when I've had such a cursed run of bad luck. I reckon I owe you about forty eight guineas, and the devil knows how I'm going to pay just at the moment, until I get my wages for this voyage."

"Don't worry" replied the younger man, "I've so much enjoyed our games, and I'm sure you will win it all back again another night."

"Never play without paying" muttered the captain, on whom the wine was having a considerable effect, "brings bad luck. Look, I'll give you a pledge."

He plunged his hand into his pocket, and brought out the small piece of velvet done up with the ribbon. He extracted the ring with some difficulty, and passed it over the table to Charles, who was now standing up. Charles took it, and looked at it carefully, and then he slipped it onto the third finger of his right hand. It fitted perfectly. Slowly that scene faded, but then Jonnie found himself looking down along the deck of the ship. But what a terrible contrast to the gently swinging lamp, for now the ship pitched and rolled in the full force of a storm, and the few sails she had set threshed about above him. The men on deck were clinging on for dear life, and the helmsman had lashed himself to the wheel.

Then Jonnies attention was suddenly caught by something ahead of the ship. A column of white spray was suddenly flung into the air a couple of hundred yards in front of the ship, and then fell back into the heaving sea. Again the spray leaped up, and Jonnie glimpsed something black and wet for a split second beneath it. In a moment of horror he realised what it was, and tried to scream a warning to the men on the deck, but no sound would come from his lips.

Then the ship struck, and chaos broke out all round him. Masts and rigging swayed, snapped, and fell, some on the deck, some into the raging sea. Another huge wave broke right over the wrecked ship, washing men into the sea, and Jonnie thought he saw the young man, Charles Hannington, leap into the sea close to the deckhouse, which had been smashed up and detached from the ship. The captain still stood by the ships wheel, clinging to the companionway post, but then another huge wave washed right over the ship, and Jonnie saw him no more.

After a short time something appeared through the spray. Jonnie peered ahead, and saw a small sandy cove, slightly sheltered, but with large waves breaking up the beach. The shoreline was covered in wreckage, among which were a number of bodies. The captain lay there, his once smart uniform torn and bedraggled; he did not move. Some yards away the young man also lay, still clinging to a piece of timber. The waves washed up to his body, but an arm moved feebly as though he was still trying to crawl further up the sand away from the cruel sea. Then Jonnie noticed a small procession of people slowly descending the winding cliff path that led down to the beach.

Again he struggled to wake himself up, but could not do so. He was aware that more time was passing.

Now the scene was a total contrast once more. Another room, but large, light and airy, lit by the winter sunlight streaming through a large window. The walls were lined with books, pictures hung there also, and in front of the window stood a large leather covered desk. Beside the desk stood two men, just entering middle age, and both dressed in smart clerical frock coats, covering waistcoats of a dark colour, with breeches and white stockings below.

"Well, this is the great day at last" said one of the men, who looked vaguely familiar to Jonnie. "I had begun to wonder if it would ever come. It's very good of you to be my best man, I must say, but watch what you say in your speech."

"Not too much about our adventures on Lundy, for example, James?" replied his companion, with a broad grin.

"Heavens, no" said James, "my mother would have a fit if she knew how near we came to falling over the cliffs there. Now, there was something I had to do before we left for the church; what on earth…Oh! Yes, I remember, I want to give you a small keepsake to remember this day, and you are not to refuse or I shall be very hurt."

James took a couple of steps over to the desk, and opened a lower drawer. From it he took out a stout cardboard box, not very big, which he placed on the desk, and then with a little difficulty lifted the lid off.

"These are some old family rings which have come down to me, and I want you to choose one for yourself to remember my wedding day."

There was some argument, with the best man gently trying to refuse such a gift, but in the end he gave way, James being quite forceful about it, and he looked closely at the rings and then selected one, and held it up.

"I'd like this one please, James," he said.

The large gold ring shone dully in the sunlight, and its single red stone seemed to glow with deep fire. Jonnie recognised it at once.

"Well, well, you've chosen the Murdering Ring" said James.

His friend nearly dropped the ring he was holding. "What?" he exclaimed.

"The murdering ring" repeated James. "My father was sent on a trip to the West Indies, when he left school. I think the idea

110

was to prospect for sources of goods for the family store in Brighton, but it was also considered a good idea that he should broaden his mind. On his way back the captain of the ship he was on discovered that he was a good card player, and insisted on playing picquet with him almost every night. In the end my father was very much the winner, apparently, and when the captain could not pay his debt, he gave my father that ring as a pledge, until he had some money and could redeem it. The next day my father asked the captain about the curious engraving on the ring, and the captain told him what he knew of its story. It seems there's some sort of a curse on the ring, and anyone who passes it on will die a violent death."

"Then I certainly won't take it from you" exclaimed his friend.

"Now my dear friend" said James gently, "you and I are Christians, and we are priests as well. We just don't believe in such superstitious nonsense, do we? Take the ring, and cancel out what evil past it may have with a bond of love. For you and I have been loving friends for a long time, haven't we, Cluppins?"

"I thought you had given up using my nickname, James, now that respectability is staring you in the face," said his friend with a smile. "Well, I will happily take the ring if you really wish me to do so, but just you take care of yourself!"

James pulled out his watch and consulted it.

"Talking of which," he said. Laughing, "I shall be in real trouble right away if you don't have me at the church on time. Blanche will slay me if I am late and then you can wave the ring at me and say 'I told you so'".

The two men turned from the window, and went out of the room, and it got darker. Time passed once again. Jonnie began to feel very hot and sweaty, but still he could not wake himself up.

The light increased now, to a cruel intensity, and he looked down as from the top of a low tree, at a clearing in the midst of a vast forest. A group of naked men were lying, bound with cords, on the ground, and they had visible wounds on their bodies. Several of them wore wooden collars of the sort carried by slaves. Around them stood a large group of fully armed native soldiers, on guard.

Then Jonnie saw a movement, and through the forest came a slow procession. Another group of soldiers were leading a white man, who looked both tired and ill. The procession stopped when it reached the clearing, and at once several of the soldiers closed in on the prisoner and began to strip his clothes off him. As they finished, the man slowly drew himself up to his full height, and made a movement with his hand. The soldiers paused, puzzled. Then the man's voice rang out loud and clear, and in English.

"Tell the King that I am about to die for the Baganda, and that I have purchased the road to Buganda with my life."

Jonnie, with a sudden sense of shock, recognised James, the Bridegroom.

James then slowly knelt down, naked in the dust and heat, and commended his soul to God. Then, suddenly nearby, a gun was fired, and at this signal the soldiers fell on all their prisoners, including James, the first Bishop of East Africa. Jonnie saw the up raised spears being driven into his body, and then he woke in a state of total terror, and with a cry of fear.

Jonnie got very drunk that night, and stayed drunk for the whole of Boxing Day, but whisky would not expunge the memories of that vivid series of dreams. Several times he was on the point of telephoning Gary to beg for the ring back, for he had begun to work out what it all meant for him. But then he had his pride, and he didn't want Gary to think he was a soft, superstitious fool.

Meanwhile, what money he had quickly evaporated, and it became imperative that he do another job, and quickly. The car needed a new starter motor, which would not come cheap, and he did not even have enough cash to fill up the petrol tank. The idea that he could not jump into his wonderful car and roar off down the road whenever he wanted to was unthinkable.

Two nights later, at about three in the morning, Jonnie swung his car left at the roundabout in Cowfold, and headed west along the A 272 for Horsham. It was a cold night, with fog patches, and possibly a bit of frost. But Jonnie was very pleased with himself. They had a much better haul this time, and he could drive a really good bargain with Gary. He glanced across at his companion, in the passenger seat, cradling the holdall with the loot in it.

Near the restaurant in West Grinsted Jonnie quickly caught up a slower moving van, and swore as he had to brake behind it. He was in a hurry, and other people had no business to be in his way at this time of night. But beyond that the road is straight, though undulating, to the traffic lights on the A 24. Jonnie waited for a couple of seconds, and then accelerated violently to overtake. The van also put on a bit of a spurt, seeing the clear, straight road ahead.

The patch of fog in the dip in the road masked the headlights of the oncoming lorry for a vital second or two, until Jonnie had reached the point of no return. Even so he might have made it, had not his wheels hit a small patch of ice on the road, just as he swerved in front of the van. He lost the back of the car, which skidded out in front of the lorry. Jonnie knew that nightmare feeling of impending disaster, over which he had no control, as he desperately spun the steering wheel in his hands. At the moment of impact, and before the darkness, the gold ring with the great red stone imprinted itself for a split second on his consciousness.

Gary read about the fatal accident in the evening paper later that same day, and at once recognised the names of the two men who had been killed. He had a very good idea, too, why they were driving towards Horsham at 3.a.m. on a foggy cold morning. He was not in the least surprised to read that the police had recovered a bag full of stolen goods from the wrecked car. But he kept his own counsel on that subject, and resolved to pass on all the items connected with Jonnie and his companion at the first opportunity. The police had a nasty habit of following up trails, and this one could possibly lead in his direction. Gary phoned up Bert Webster, a very useful contact who among other things ran an antiques and bric-a-brac stall in a market near the Elephant and Castle in East London. That was a pleasant distance away from the domain of the Sussex Police.

Next morning Gary bundled up the items he wished to part with, together with a few others, and drove up to town. He had several business visits he wished to make, but he went and found Bert first of all, and after a good deal of haggling accepted a ridiculously low price for the items. Why, the gold ring with the large red stone must be worth a couple of hundred on its own to the right person. But Gary was in a hurry, and Bert, while suffering the after effects of a hard nights drinking, was very obstinate.

Gary returned home in a bad frame of mind, and took it out on his wife and young children.

In March Gary decided to create a water garden. It was something he had wanted to do for some time, but his wife had always objected to the idea on the grounds that ponds would be dangerous for the children. A lot of nonsense. Why, Wayne was nearly six, and Samantha nearly four, bless her. Gary decided he would now do just as he pleased, and curtly informed his long suffering wife that the children's safety was her responsibility. He then took himself off to the large garden centre in Crawley, and spent a large amount of money. He returned with pond liners, a pump and lengths of cable, water lilies in pots, and some fish. In the meantime his gardener was instructed to dig the main pond, and pile the earth in a mound beside it, to make a future waterfall. For two days Gary supervised his project, bringing in quantities of stones, building the waterfall, and laying the hose to the top of the mound, and the cable to the pump, which he brought in through a hole near the window and the passed under the carpet to a power point near the fireplace. He knew it was not the right way to go about it, but it was the easiest, and he liked the idea of being able to sit in his armchair and switch on his fountain and waterfall without even having to move.

Gary was quite thrilled when it worked first time, and there seemed to be no serious leaks. He then set to work to stock it with the plants and fish, while the long suffering gardener was bidden to get busy with more plants and ferns to surround it. By early April, with some bulbs in flower, it really did look very nice. Gary was immensely proud of it, and his wife had an unending job keeping the children away.

On a sunny afternoon in late April Gary was standing admiring it all for the hundredth time. Yet the fountain did not appear to be quite as good as it had been. He knelt down on the grass, reached with difficulty across to the pump, and adjusted the valve. No improvement resulted, and he then noticed that the pump filter was clogged with weed. Gary got up and swore loudly. Why was there always more work to be done? For the moment he forgot that the whole enterprise had been his own brainchild. He stumped indoors, leaving a lot of mud on the carpet, and switched off the pump at the wall socket. Then he went back outside and lay down by the edge of the pond. He reached down underwater and tried to detach the pump filter. It was stuck, and the cable was in the way. He grabbed at the cable in a rage, forgetting that he had had problems attaching it in the first place. It came away in his hand.

As Gary began his tussle with the pump, Samantha toddled into the living room, and being unsupervised for a minute or two, headed straight for the television and turned it on by pressing its button. But nothing happened. She looked at it for a few seconds. Then she remembered. Grown ups sometimes had to turn on a switch thing over by the fireplace. Samantha toddled over there, and gazed at the two switches, sitting side by side. Then she dropped on her knees, and after a couple of seconds thought, she reached out and pushed down one of the switches.

As Samantha was facing the wall, she did not see her father catapulted into the air, as the electric shock ripped through every nerve in his body, magnified by the water, and she did not see him thrown forward to land with a splash in the pond, scattering the fish in all directions. Samantha looked in disappointment at the blank television, and then tried the other switch. This time it worked.

Later, the coroner could not decide whether it was the shock which killed Gary, or whether he drowned soon afterwards in his pond. It did not really matter. His wife had the pond filled in immediately, for the children's safety, and within six months she had moved to a new house with a new husband.

Bert Webster never saw the announcement of Gary's death, but then his only use for newspapers was wrapping up fish and chips. Business was very bad that year, and as a result Bert became very depressed. Various creditors began to hound him, and as a result he took to drinking even more heavily than usual. It was a fine evening in September when Bert staggered out of the pub up the road from his market stall, clutching a full bottle of whisky. For once he had had quite a good day, but now he was vaguely conscious that instead of using the profit he had made to pay off some of his most pressing debts, he had drunk most of it. He stood uncertainly on the pavement, and remembered that he had even managed to sell that damned gold ring, that had been hanging about for weeks.

A young chap, who said he was a builder's labourer, had surprisingly taken a fancy to it. Bert moved slowly down the pavement, until he came to a bench which faced a small green, and there he sat down with a bump, and opened the bottle of whisky. There was very little left in the bottle when a policeman found him lying down on the ground behind the bench about three in the morning. He was pronounced dead on arrival at the hospital, and the cause of death was given as alcohol poisoning, which was immediately apparent to anyone who got within six feet of his still body.

Stephen was delighted with his ring. He rubbed it vigorously on his jeans, and admired it on his finger. It fitted to perfection, and that old chap on the stall had assured him it would be a good investment, might even bring him good luck! Much more interesting than sticking your money away in a building society, that is, assuming you had any. Stephen seldom did.

Stephen decided he would wear his new ring all the time. It would impress his girlfriend. He might even give it to her if she came up to scratch soon! He wore it to work the next day, and showed it to his mates, who were impressed. It was a real treasure, Stephen declared. It would change his luck. He whistled as he pranced along the scaffolding high above the ground, showing off as usual, and ignoring all the firm's safety regulations for men working in such situations. But he, Stephen, would never fall off, and the ring on his finger was surely going to change his future!

I happen to be one of the very few people in the world who have handled the Murdering Ring, but fortunately I never possessed it myself. I wonder what it is up to now?

NINE.   THE YOUNG PRINCE.

The sun rose as usual into a clear blue sky, and its rays picked out the tops of pillars, roofs and immense statues in the temples at Thebes and Karnak. As the sun rose higher, the whole of the great city basked in its light, and away to the west the waters of the Nile began to glisten and dance. Egrets, Herons and other birds were up early, wading along looking for fish in the slowly moving water. Horns sounded from the Temples, as the Priests were called to attend the hour of sacrifice One or two boats cast off from the bank of the river, and moved across the stream, propelled by paddles. The noise of stone masons and carpenters began to be heard. The east bank of the river was coming to new and vibrant life with the dawning of another day.

Across the river, on the west bank, there seemed to be a total contrast. There was, it is true, an elaborate landing stage, but beyond that there very few houses to be seen, and then the desert began stretching away into the distance, unbroken, until it merged with the reddish brown mountains on the horizon, now beginning to be lit up by the harsh rays of the sun. It was a desolate scene compared with the bustling city on the other bank, and appropriately so, for the business of the western bank was death.

In some long past century, a Pharaoh had stood with his back to the great temple at Thebes, and gazed out across the river to the distant mountains. Their tranquility, and solid permanence had moved him, and he forthwith decreed that his own tomb should be prepared out there for him, at a spot of his own choosing. Without further delay he had himself rowed across the river in a ceremonial barge, and then carried up towards the mountains on a litter carried by slaves. From beneath its rich canopy he looked about him. It was hot and desolate, but the Pharaoh was very determined, and at length he found his chosen spot in a rocky valley that sloped upwards into the foothills. At once a huge force of slaves, with their overseers, was recruited, presided over by the Pharaohs own personal architect, and then the arduous work of tunneling began.

Fortunately the rock in that area proved ideal for the enterprise, being strong to support tunnels and arched chambers, but not over hard. The final proof of the blessing of the Gods came when the completion of the tomb and the death of the Pharaoh almost completely coincided. His son and heir at once gave orders for the beginning of his own tomb, having chosen a spot not far from his father's tomb. Down the succeeding centuries, as Pharaoh followed Pharaoh, the number of tombs in the Valley of the Kings grew steadily, and each one was designed to be more magnificent and secure than any of its predecessors. On the west bank of the river a huge funeral industry developed, which centred on the great work of preparing royal tombs. The current ruler would be constantly popping across the river to see how his own final resting place was getting on!

In a small hut, in one of the many villages that now were strung out along the west bank of the river Nile, Hora stirred and looked at his shadow on the wall opposite. It was high time he got up from sleep, and he tossed off his covering and sprang up from his sleeping mat. He was aged fourteen, just entering manhood. He was already quite tall, and with his bronzed skin, dark hair and handsome face he would be a very striking man one day in the not too distant future. But now he must hurry, gather a few scraps of his mother's bread, put some water into a gourd, and hasten to join the column of men and women already winding out of the village, and heading towards the west. The power of the sun on their backs could be felt more and more strongly.

After a brisk walk of nearly two hours, Hora arrived at his place of work. Everything appeared to be just as he had left it the day before, yet this was to be a day of great significance for him, had he but known it. Egypt at this time was ruled by a great Pharaoh, with a most beautiful queen. The Pharaoh was in the prime of life, and it was expected that he would live and rule his people for many years. He had two sons, which was a great blessing from the Gods. The elder one was about seventeen years old, and already famed for his abilities throughout Egypt. His younger brother was just fifteen. Men did not seem to say a lot about him or what he did.

Hora's work place was not very much to look at from the outside, being just a hole in the rocky hillside. The entrance was about eight feet high, and six feet wide. This was to be the tomb eventually of the Pharaoh's eldest son, Amnon-Ra. True, it was sincerely hoped that it would not be required for many a long year, but it was to be truly magnificent as would befit a great Pharaoh, and work on it would take many decades. So far the entrance shaft and the main chamber had been hewn out of the rock, and side chambers had been planned and begun. Hora clambered into the entrance, and began to descend the shaft. At once it became blessedly cooler, although the quality of the air diminished. Hora came to the main chamber, and reported himself to the overseer, who was waiting there. His name was marked on a tablet, and he was given his small rush light, and a pot of oil so that he could tend it during the day. He moved over to the further wall of the main chamber, and found his paints where he had left them. He would need some more fresh water, and he went to collect some from a large jar near the bottom of the shaft. Then he settled down to his work. He could not really remember when it was discovered that he had this talent for painting. It was certainly inherited from his father, who was now working on the Pharaoh's own tomb, situated about a mile away, and who was regarded as a most important artist.

Hora had to prepare the wall for a huge mural of a hunting scene, fit for a great Prince of Egypt. He carefully mixed the ochre and green paints in the right proportions, and happily set to work on the occupation he loved. About noon a buzz of conversation was heard, and a man came quickly down the main entrance stairway, and spoke excitedly to the overseer. The overseer looked startled, and then began to go round the chambers, talking to his workmen. Presently he came to Hora, busily painting. For a few moments he paused and looked up at the work in progress. Then he said quietly,

"This is a great day for us, Hora. His Highness, the great Prince Amnon-Ra is now coming to inspect our work. You will stand by your work when he comes to you, and only speak when you are spoken to. Is that understood?"

"Yes" whispered Hora. The instruction was hardly necessary, as he was completely tongue tied already at the very thought of the wonderful visitation which would soon take place.

About an hour later the Prince arrived, with his retinue, and accompanied by his younger brother. Hora at once laid down his brush and paint, and stood to attention beside the large wall. By the vastly increased light of many torches, he was able to watch proceedings. First the Prince talked to his overseer, and another man whom Hora guessed to be the architect, while his younger brother looked all round him. They were looking then at a plan, and the older Prince kept looking round the chamber, as though trying to get his bearings. Hora could hardly take his eyes off the prince. It was not the splendour of his clothing, for compared with his brother he was quite simply dressed, and with very little ornament. It was his face and his bearing which so forcibly struck Hora. In contrast to his younger brother, who was stocky and fleshy, with a greasy sort of look about him, the Prince Amnon-Ra was tall, with a finely proportioned body, a laughing mouth, and clear blue eyes which seemed to take in all around him. Once or twice he laughed at something that was said to him. His whole being radiated humour, courage and health. Any man would gladly lay down his life for such a

Prince, and Hora's heart swelled with pride as he remembered that he was indeed working for this great man. His painting could be a source of inspiration for this Prince. He stole a glance at the rock wall behind him, and then let his imagination run on to imagine the scene which he would depict on it. What an honour his work would be.

The Prince and his retinue began to move round the chamber. His brother made it very obvious that he was already totally bored with the whole business. Hora's heart beat faster. At length the Prince arrived in front of his wall, and stood looking critically up at it.

"What scene is to be here?" he asked the architect.

"A hunting scene, Highness," was the reply.

"Ah, yes" said the Prince. Then he turned to Hora.

"What is your name?"

"Hora, your Highness" whispered Hora.

"You are very young to be undertaking such an important work, are you not?"

"I will do my very best, Highness."

"Tell me, what do you plan for this scene?"

Hora swallowed twice, and began to speak in a voice which did not seem at all like his own.

"I plan to have your Highness here, mounted on a fine black horse, and with three of your friends beside you, and with other huntsmen behind. You will carry a bow and arrows. Then, in front of you, will be a fine brown water buck, panting at the end of the chase. Beyond him, and perhaps splashing through some water, will be three more smaller buck. Above them will be a flock of duck, taking to flight, with green heads, but one will already be in the mouth of one of your hunting dogs. The other dogs will be running beside your horse."

Hora stopped for breath, acutely conscious that his tongue had run away with him. His enthusiasm for his craft had quite spilled over. The overseer was looking a bit worried. There was a long silence as the Prince looked at the wall, as though he could see the finished picture already.

Then the Prince turned round and looked at Hora again.

"I love my hunting, Hora," he said quietly. "Did you already know that? Paint this picture just as you have described it, and paint it well, for it will be a great joy to me both in this life and in the great afterlife. It will provide me with both food and the excitement of the chase once again. I shall come back again very soon to see how it is progressing. Yes, paint it just as you have described it to me."

"Yes, I will try my best, Highness" whispered Hora, and his heart was nearly bursting with pride.

In the following weeks and months Hora worked with increased dedication on his painting. Even the overseer was impressed, and often strolled over to look at it. He finished the background for the sky and the distant hills, and began work on the water. In the villages at night there were stories about a great campaign to be waged by Pharaoh and his armies against enemies in the north east.

Hora completed the first coats of paint on the water, and began work on the land which would support the horses. Pharaoh had led a great army, it was said, across the border out of Egypt to extend his realm and capture booty from his enemies. Both his sons were accompanying their father on this great expedition. Hora began to draw in the horses, and to outline the positions of the other animals. He resolved to leave the Prince to the very last. The overseer complained about all the paint Hora was using, but in fact he was hugely impressed with the work, and was only teasing the boy. He kept coming back to admire the great painting, and to marvel at its colour and detail. Hora was given a second rush light, so that he could see better to execute the more detailed work.

The Egyptian army, men said, was making really good progress, reaching out towards the great rivers in the east. They had won several small battles against forces sent against them. They penetrated deeper into enemy territory, with increasing confidence. Hora drew in the positions of the hunting dogs, and for the flying duck.

When the blow fell, it came without any warning at all, out of a clear sky. A messenger, covered in dust and sweat, came dashing down the entrance passage, staggered across to the overseer, fell on his knees and grasped the man's robe. The overseer listened to the gasped out message, and turned white with shock. For what seemed like an age he stood like a statue. Then he called all the workmen, who had stopped work as one man, to come over to him at once. Hora put down his brush, and ran over with the others. The messenger was given water, and sat on a low bench.

"I have grave news of great horror to impart to you all" said the overseer. "Give them your message" he said to the messenger.

The messenger stood up shakily, and said

"Our great army has been ambushed by the cunning enemy. They had not the courage to fight us in open battle. Now Pharaoh himself has been slain in the battle, while fighting with great courage, and his eldest son, the mighty Prince Amnon-Ra had also been slain as he tried to defend his father. Only the younger prince has escaped. The army is in flight back to Egypt. If they can bring back the body of our beloved Prince, then this, his tomb will be required very shortly. This is my message."

There was a stunned silence, and at length the overseer said in a voice filled with sorrow

"You have heard the message. We must press on with the work with all possible speed. What cannot be done in time, must be left undone. Now go back, each man to his work as appointed."

Hora dragged himself back to his wall, utterly numb from shock. All the light and inspiration had gone from his life and his work. Without any enthusiasm he continued to draw in the flying duck.

Around Hora the activity in the tomb increased tenfold. Chambers were hurriedly completed, their walls left rough hewn. In what was truly record time, a sarcophagus was constructed in the burial chamber, and all the burial furnishings began to arrive. Craftsmen for miles around worked day and night to try and meet the deadline set them. The overseer offered to try and find other painters to assist Hora, but he vehemently declined the offer. The picture he was painting would be his, and his alone. He alone had discussed its details with the great prince when he had visited. Anyway, good painters were in very short supply, for his father and many others were desperately trying to finish the Pharaoh's great tomb at the same time. The appalling double tragedy had taken them all by surprise.

Hora hardly slept at all by night. Thoughts tumbled over one another in his brain throughout the hours of darkness, but gradually as the frantic days passed he formulated a plan, a plan born of pure desperation. It was obvious to him that unless he rushed his work to the point where all quality of painting was abandoned, there was no way his masterpiece would be finished in time. Yet he still would not let another man lay a finger on his work. The very idea was anathema to him. The overseer had warned him that at any moment from now on the mourners might arrive bearing the Prince's body, for it had been confirmed by messengers that they were on their way. Then any work unfinished would have to be left just as it was.

Hora began to take a much greater interest in what was going on around him. He watched the way that furniture was being stacked, or rather dumped. He noticed the places where food and water were secreted. He carefully noted the pile of rush lights and supply of oil to light the young Prince along the path to his new life. Three more days passed, and anyone observing

Hora as he worked would have been surprised and perplexed to see that he exhibited none of the signs of near panic to be found among those on all sides. Instead, he worked slowly and painstakingly on his work, and the details of the great hunting scene took shape slowly. The overseer, after passing a few remarks, left him alone. He had much to do and plenty of other chaotic things to try and sort out.

Then at last messengers arrived to say, in sorrowful tones, that the royal cortege was approaching the tomb. The wailing of the mourners began to be heard, even down in the main chamber, and it was mixed with the echoing blasts from the funeral horns. All eyes were on the entrance to the chamber, down which the Prince would be born to his final resting place. No-one noticed Hora, as, moving like a shadow, he clutched his precious rush light and slid behind a stack of furniture at the far side of the chamber. No-one saw him drop to the ground and crawl under some long wooden stools, covered in still drying gilt paint. No-one noticed his absence, as pandemonium reigned in the tomb, with mourners and masons getting in each others way in the dim light.

The coffin containing the mummified body was reverently put in its appointed place, walls were finally completed, and then the burial chamber itself was bricked up. More furniture arrived, somewhat to the overseer's surprise, and this was stacked in an untidy heap in the main chamber. Nobody quite knew what it was intended to do, but they put it there just in case. The flickering torches cast the shadows of animal statues in weird shapes on the stone walls. Then the living began to leave the tomb, and the lights began to go out as they moved to the entrance passageway, and began to brick up the door. Hora lay very still in his hiding place, cradling his rush light, and comforted by its tiny flame. Outside the noise made by the stonemasons gradually diminished, and soon it was obvious they had withdrawn to the outer entrance, and were blocking that up also. The noise of their mallets reverberated round the tomb, and Hora remained very still in his hiding place.

It was thirst which eventually caused him to move, crawling back out, and to go in search of water. Hora had to wrestle a great deal with his conscience when it came to this part of his plan. Would he be stealing from his beloved Prince if he helped himself to food and water from the supplies left in the tomb? He finally reasoned that so long as he was engaged about the Prince's business, his highness would understand. Having refreshed himself with food and water, he sought out two more rush lights from the stock left, and lit them from his own precious flame. Now he not only had a lot more light, but he had a back up for safety's sake. He also took a small jar of oil with him, and established a sort of camp in front of his picture. He collected his paints, and set them out in order, and then, having listened for a few moments to the far distant noise of the masons at work, he resumed painting his great masterpiece. It would indeed be the finest picture of which he was capable, so that his beloved Prince would enjoy the best of hunting in the great afterlife.

Hora began to paint in the magnificent horses, and became so immersed in his work that he hardly noticed when the noises of work from outside the tomb finally stopped. Now there was nothing in the world to disturb his concentration, just a silence so deep that even the quiet sound of a brush on the wall seemed like an intrusion. Sometimes while he was working he sang quietly to himself. When he was tired he lay down on a convenient mat, and slept, having carefully tended his lamps. He ate very little, and just lived for his painting. The horses were now finished, and the leaping buck were begun. Once or twice, as he looked at his creation in the lamp light, at the buck dashing through the blue sparkling water, he felt a great longing for the fresh air and the sun, but he suppressed it, and returned steadfastly to his task. The buck were now finished, and he turned his attention to the dogs and the duck. The dogs did present difficulties, and he made one or two small errors, but they were quickly and carefully corrected. The ducks were the fattest he could imagine, and must have had some difficulty becoming airborne!

It was about the time that Hora was finishing the duck that he began to feel a drowsiness that stole over him from time to time. It seemed to be worst when he was standing up on a stool to tackle the highest parts of the painting. If he then lay down on his mat, and had a drink of water, he found the faintness would go away quite quickly. He wondered where the smoke from his rush lights went to. Perhaps somewhere they had built a secret ventilation shaft to the outside. If that was the case, certainly no light penetrated to the tomb. Hora put the idea from him, and turned once again to his picture.

Now, he started work on the human figures in the scene, keeping his Prince to be the last to be painted. The Prince's retinue, and the huntsmen, took their places in the pageant, all suitably attired in magnificent clothing. Hora began to feel faint more frequently, and lay for longer curled up on his mat. The water began to taste rather brackish, and it did not revive him so well as before. The jar of oil became exhausted, and though he searched carefully he could only find one other small one, and that was only half full. He lit two more rush lights, as he was having difficulty in seeing properly, and he wanted all his faculties to be at a peak as he tackled the most important part of his painting.

He began work on the Prince himself, when everything else in the vast mural was complete. It was a sort of reward for his perseverance, keeping the best until last. But now he found it was not at all easy. He had such a vision of his great hero, that capturing him in paint was well nigh impossible. Given a limited stock of paints, - now much diminished, and the poor light, in spite of five rush lights. And then the dizziness got worse, until he was having to lie down every few minutes, or he would have fallen.

Finally, it was only the noble, laughing face that had to be completed, for Hora was determined that his Prince would look happy and excited in this scene depicting his favourite sport. He lay on the floor, feeling terribly weak, and tried to remember just how the Prince had looked on that momentous day when he had first seen the picture. But for some reason Hora's brain did not seem to focus properly any longer. When he dragged himself up, and picked up his brush and paint pot, his ideas became all jumbled up. Then, suddenly, as though he was looking out through a window, his thoughts cleared, and he saw his Prince standing clearly and vividly before him. Working quickly now, he captured the shape of the face, those brilliant blue eyes, the fine nose, and the laughing mouth, all surrounded by the flowing hair. It was indeed his Prince, and no one who knew him could possibly mistake him. A few final small brush strokes, and then the faintness swirled back, and he very nearly fell from the stool. He staggered across to his mat again, and almost collapsed onto it, dropping his brush.

Then he noticed that one of his lights had gone out, and another was flickering a lot, always a bad sign. He ought to tend them, and find some more oil from somewhere, but not just now. He glanced up, and saw that the painting was complete, finished. He slept.

When Hora awoke, he thought at first that it was completely dark, and a terrible panic rose up inside his chest. Then he saw that one of his rush lights was still burning, and gradually he relaxed. Then slowly he turned over, and with great difficulty raised his head. Above him, dimly seen, was his great masterpiece in all its glory. Horses and riders, huntsmen and fleeing buck, leaping dogs and the duck in flight. It was indeed finished. And as Hora looked at it, the Princes eyes seemed to fasten on his own, and the Prince laughed in pure excitement and joy. Hora had to lower his head, to try and conquer the faintness that was engulfing him again. He lay and looked at the tiny flame of the one rush light. He really must get up and tend it, find some more oil from somewhere. He would get up in a minute or two, when he felt a little stronger. In a minute or two.

The tiny flame flickered again, and went out.

Some time later Hora became aware of a light in the chamber, coming from the corner of the roof above the entrance doorway. It must be the ventilation shaft, which he had not noticed, though it was really very bright. Hora decided to try and get nearer to investigate it, and he found to his surprise that he could move more easily than he expected. He found that the light increased as he moved towards the mouth of the shaft. He almost seemed to be floating, and looking back now he could see every detail of the great painting on the wall behind him. But it was again the Prince's eyes which held his, and the Prince's hand almost seemed to beckon to him. Hora found himself moving to the entrance of the shaft, and then going further inside it. The light was even brighter now, and how wonderful to see the sun again, and to feel the cool waters of the river Nile on hot and dusty feet.

At the far end of the shaft Hora saw a figure bathed in the light, - in fact it almost seemed that the figure was the source of the light. As Hora moved closer, the figure began to seem familiar to him. With a growing sense of wonder and joy, recognition dawned on him, and as the man in front of him opened his arms in welcome, Hora knew beyond all doubt that it was his Prince. Then he was enveloped in an embrace of pure love. "Your Highness," said Hora in a whisper, after time had passed, "I have finished your hunting picture."

The Prince laughed, that wonderful and familiar laugh again.

"I am not 'Your Highness' any longer, Hora," he said. "Look at yourself now, beloved, and see how you have reaped the true and eternal reward of your faithfulness."

Then Hora looked down at himself, and he realised that he too had become a Prince.

TEN. TO DIE IN BED.

The telephone rang in the smart detached house on the outskirts of Ipswich, and Diana glanced up instinctively at the kitchen clock as she reached across the ironing board and picked up the cordless receiver from its stand. It was just on 6.p.m.

"Hullo" she said, brightly.

"Hullo, darling" replied a rather weary voice.

"I take it you've finished now?"

"Yes, at long last" said her husband, Steve.

"You sound really tired" said Diana, "why don't you stay down there in a hotel for the night. Tomorrow is Saturday, so you can perfectly well drive back in the morning. The firm can certainly afford to pay a hotel bill or two."

"You know I always like to sleep in my own bed," responded her husband, rather testily. "I'll get a sandwich at a garage, and hopefully be home by ten, if the traffic isn't too bad."

"Drive carefully" said his wife, sympathetically. She knew there was absolutely no point in arguing, especially when Steve was tired, so she put down the 'phone and resumed her ironing. Her son would be home from his holiday job any time now, so she would have company for the evening, at any rate. Steve was funny about being away from home. He had this fixation about dying in his own bed.

"Don't ever let them shunt me into a hospital" he'd say, quite fiercely when he was in one of his morbid moods, "the only place I want to die is in my own bed."

Diana was beginning to feel the whole matter was becoming an obsession with Steve, and she tried to avoid the subject completely if she could.

Somewhere on the outskirts of Southampton Steve pulled into a garage, and filled up his Mondeo with petrol. He also bought a packet of sandwiches, a bar of chocolate, and a bottle of Coke. Then he settled himself back into his car, ate a couple of bits of chocolate, opened the sandwiches and put them on the seat beside him, had a swig from the bottle, turned on his radio, and headed off towards the M.27.

The prospect of a Friday night drive up the motorways and the A 12 was not a pleasant one. He swung the car up the slip road onto the M.27, and almost immediately began to position himself in the correct lane to move left onto the M3 for London. Ahead of him an older blue car was also moving up the slip road, and Steve moved out and accelerated to overtake on the dual carriageway. Thank goodness he knew the route very well indeed.

Diana heard her son Paul come in through the back door, and called out to him. He came through into the kitchen, and gave his mother a kiss on the cheek. He was a tall boy, with longish brown hair, blue eyes, and a rather sallow complexion. He had been fortunate, and got a good job repairing televisions and other electrical goods during the university vacation. It was ideal for him, as he was studying electrical engineering at university, and any practical experience would be a help with his course.

"Any news from Dad?" he asked his mother.

"He rang about twenty minutes ago," replied Diana, "and he said he was leaving the office shortly. I do so wish he didn't have to do these ghastly long evening journeys when he is so tired by the end of the week."

"Dad'll be O.K." said Paul, trying to sound bright and confident. "You know what he's like about trying to get home for the night no matter where he is."

"Yes, I know," said his mother, with a sigh. "We'll go ahead and have supper. I'll get it ready as soon as I've finished this pile of ironing. I always like to get it done and out of my sight before the weekend. If you want to go and have a bath, this would be a good time."

"Good idea" said her son, and picking up the daily paper he headed off in the direction of the stairs.

Diana was not unduly worried when ten o'clock came and went. The traffic must have been particularly bad. She tried to watch the beginning of the news, but couldn't really concentrate. She felt very tired, almost depressed, for some reason. This was unusual at the start of a weekend. As a rule the prospect of seeing Steve, and having two whole glorious days with him acted as a good pick-me-up. She decided to have a long bath, in company with lots of rich smelling bath salts, and she began to run the water in their bathroom.

Perhaps it was because of the sound of the running water that Diana never heard Steve's car come in, or the sound of the automatic garage door open and shut. He suddenly appeared through the door from the utility room, just as she was about to turn out the kitchen light and go up to her bath. Paul had already retired to his bedroom and his own television and computer. Steve stood there, looking all in. She was at once very concerned about him.

"Welcome home, darling" she exclaimed warmly, moving towards him.

"Must go to the loo" he mumbled, without really looking at her. He went past her, and out into the hall, and she heard the door of the cloakroom latch. She suddenly remembered that she had left the bath running, and she hurried upstairs to turn off the taps. The bath could wait a few minutes. She came down again, and Steve was at the kitchen table leafing through the letters that had arrived during the day, and which she had put there for him.

"Can I get you something to eat?" she asked him solicitously, "scrambled eggs or something light?"

"I don't really feel like anything now," he responded wearily.

"I expect you're just too tired to feel hungry" said Diana. "What about a hot drink of some sort?"

"Not just at present" Steve answered. "You go and have your bath, and I'll follow you in a few minutes when I've looked at one or two of these letters. I need to spend a few moments unwinding. You know what it's like driving these days."

Diana left him rather reluctantly, and went upstairs to her bath. He did look very pale, but it was probably just over tiredness. It would be awful if he was hatching 'flu, with a busy weekend ahead, and people coming in to dinner on Saturday night. And there was also so much to be done in the garden as well. She undressed in their bedroom, and then went along and got into her delicious bath.

Steve did not appear, but she could hear him going round the house making sure all the windows and doors were secure, as he always did. Paul was obviously still up, and she could hear his stereo playing at quite a reasonable volume for once, in his bedroom. As she was drying herself, Steve put his head round the bathroom door and said he was going to undress and put his dressing gown on, and would she kindly run him a bath.

"Are you quite sure that you don't want me to make you a hot drink now?" Diana asked him, but he just shook his head wearily, and went along to their bedroom. By the time she got there he had undressed, and in fact they passed in the doorway.

"Don't go to sleep in the bath" she said lightly. "I shall come back to check up in ten minutes, to make sure you haven't drowned!"

"No chance of that" he said, rather morosely, she thought. "I do hope to goodness it's not the 'flu" she repeated to herself, as she climbed into the bed. She tried to read for a few minutes until he came and joined her, but the book fell from her hand, and she was hardly aware of his return to the bedroom. She heard him sigh deeply as he sat down on the bed and then rolled sideways in the curious manner he always followed, pulling the duvet on top of himself. She waited for him to move across to kiss her, and when he did not, she stretched a leg out in his direction. It encountered his thigh, which seemed cold.

"He can't have had a hot bath after all" she thought, and she tried to summon up the strength to make a comment, to ask how he was feeling now. But now sleep overwhelmed her, and she never managed even to say goodnight.

It was a brighter morning when she awoke, and she opened one eye and watched the pattern the newly risen sun made on the flowered wallpaper, for a minute or two. Then she remembered it was a Saturday, and she gave a little sigh of contentment. There was no need to hurry, because no-one had to rush off to work. She rolled over gently in the bed, so as not to disturb Steve. At least he must have slept well, for she had not been aware of him at all during the night, which was unusual. He was quite right, she reflected. There was indeed no substitute for one's own bed. She raised her head a little to look at him. The other side of the bed was empty.

"Why on earth has he got up so early?" she asked herself. She lay and turned over in her own mind various possible explanations. Perhaps he had gone down to make them both a cup of tea. But that was very unlike him, it was she who usually made the first cup of tea. Was he not feeling well? But then surely he would have said something, and sensibly stayed in bed? Could there be some early appointment he had forgotten to tell her about? But again, that was very unlikely on a Saturday morning. On an impulse, she leaned over and felt his side of the bed. She expected it to be still warm, but it was cold, almost clammy to the touch. Whenever Steve had got up, it had been a long time ago.

Diana felt vaguely uneasy, as one does when in the presence of the unexplained. She got out of bed, put on her dressing gown, and went downstairs to the kitchen. She expected to find Steve there, perhaps having an early breakfast to make up for having eaten nothing the night before. But the kitchen was quite empty, and she looked for a note in vain. They often left one another notes on the corner of the table. In fact, the kitchen was exactly as she had left it the night before, with a few pieces of crockery drying in the rack on the draining board, and a magazine she had glanced at still lying open on the table. She stood in the doorway, holding on to the door handle, and desperately trying to piece together the components of this jigsaw puzzle. It was all really unlike Steve. And now she came to think of it, he had behaved rather oddly the night before.

Supposing he had left them? The thought, forcing itself upon her against her will, made her grip the door handle more tightly. One heard of such things happening much too often. It had been the case with Hetty and her husband less than a year ago. No word of warning at all: just "I'm afraid it's all over between us. There's someone else, you see, has been for several years. It's one of the secretaries at work."

Yet surely there would have been some sign, some premonition? Only last week Steve had brought her back a lovely bunch of flowers. Did that indicate the strength of his love for her, or was it an attempt to still a very guilty conscience? Perhaps Paul would have a clue, - after all he had been still up when she went to bed. She went slowly back upstairs. Diana knocked softly on his door, and received a muffled reply. Not surprising, this was a very early hour for Paul on a Saturday. She opened the door, and put her head round it.

"Paul, dad seems to have got up early for some reason" she said, trying to keep the worry out of her voice. "Any ideas where he might be? He didn't say anything to you last night before he came to bed?"

Paul said "No mum, 'fraid not."

"I'll have a look round and see where he's got to" said Diana, with an optimism which she did not feel. "He's so silly not to have given himself a proper lie in after such a long day yesterday."

She went slowly round the house, upstairs and downstairs, looking carefully into each room, saying his name from time to time, and rather fearful of what she might find. But everything was exactly as she had left it the night before. She returned to her bedroom, and threw on the first clothes that came to hand. There must be a simple explanation for the apparent mystery, some obvious factor she had overlooked.

She looked out of the back bedroom window. It was a truly lovely morning now. Suppose he had had the urge to get out into the garden. He knew what a lot of work needed doing, - she had reminded him by presenting him with a list only a couple of days before. Convinced that at last she had found the solution to it all, and with a lighter heart, she went down to the front door, and out into the fairly extensive garden. She turned right, heading for the main garden down the side and to the rear of the house. There was no sign of Steve, and it was honestly not the sort of garden a man could hide in, even if he had wanted to. The door of the garden shed was shut, and bolted from the outside, as it should be. She did not bother to unbolt it and look inside.

Only one other place remained, then, and that was the garage. Diana went across to the side door that led in from the garden. It was locked. She went back into the house through the back door, and then through the utility room. The inside door into the garage was unlocked, as it had been when Steve had arrived home the previous night. This looked more hopeful, yet it was with a cold fear in her heart that she opened the door, and turned on the garage light. The most significant thing in their tidy garage was at one revealed for all to see. There was only one car inside, and it was her own small runabout. Steve's car, the dark red Mondeo, was missing. Diana stood and stared at the scene, trying to work out the answer. Steve must have gone out, but why? At that moment Paul appeared by her side, looking as though he had also dressed very quickly.

"Where on earth can dad have gone off to at this time of day, and on Saturday?" asked Diana.

Paul shrugged his shoulders. "I never heard the car start up," he said, "and I usually hear the garage door from my room when it opens and shuts, 'cos it creaks."

"I'm going to make myself a cup of coffee" said Diana, suddenly feeling rather unsteady. "I'll make you one at the same time."

She went back into the kitchen and put the kettle on. Paul joined her, and sat on a stool at the table. It was a comfort to have him there.

"I just can't understand dad" said Diana, a little petulantly now, for deep down she was filled with a strange fear. "You know how he is always saying how he loves his bed, and he even wants to die there, of all the ridiculous things. It isn't like him to do something like this. He hasn't even left a note on the table, as we always do for one another."

She handed Paul his cup of coffee, and sat down with her own. A car drew up outside the house.

"Here he is" said Paul.

"Well" said his mother, "He's going to get a real earful when he comes through that door." But her voice had a lighter tone, as relief flooded into her body.

The front door bell rang.

"Now what?" said Diana.

"Must have forgotten his door key" said Paul.

Diana got up and moved towards the door. "It's on his ring with his car keys" she said, "he can't possible forget it, or lose it."

She went down the hall to the front door, and opened it rather slowly.

A policeman, in uniform, was standing on the doorstep.

"Mrs Rothman?" he asked.

"Yes" replied Diana, all her apprehension returning.

"May I come in, please?"

She led the way into the hall, and then turned to face him. He seemed ill at ease.

"I'm afraid I have to give you bad news, Mrs Rothman" he said. Paul had come to stand in the kitchen doorway.

"Is it my husband?" Diana managed to ask.

"I'm afraid so" said the policeman. "It has taken us a long time to do the identification." Diana looked very bewildered.

"It happened where you leave the M.27 and join the M3. An idiot driver got on the wrong motorway, and then as far as we can tell pulled right over in front of your husband's car. He was forced to swerve, and went over the bank onto the motorway below, the one he had just left. His car turned over, and a lorry went over it, and left it crushed and on fire.

"But that can't be…." began Diana.

"It took the Fire Brigade a long time to get your husband out, and we couldn't get reliable identification of the car until this morning."

"But my husband was home here last night," cried Diana, relief flooding through her. "You must have made a terrible mistake."

Now it was the policeman's turn to look bewildered. He fished in the pocket of his uniform, and produced a bunch of keys. Slowly and rather reluctantly he held them out to Diana. They were burned and twisted with the extreme heat they had been subjected to, but the small silver metal tag with the St. Christopher medal on it, which Diana had given to Steve when he got the new car, was clearly to be seen.

Diana took the keys in her hand, as if in a dream, and stared at them. "Determined to die in his own bed; must get home at all costs." The words echoed through her whirling brain. Steve had come home to die, then, even though he was already…..

140

Fifteen Love

Diana took a half step forward, clutching the bunch of keys, and the policeman caught her as she fell.

ELEVEN. A NAVAL OCCASION.

Andrew Rushmore might well have been described as a recluse. The two most significant events in his life, which had spanned fifty six years, were his Service in the Royal Navy before, during and after the Second World War, and the dropping of a German bomb on his home in Portsmouth in November 1942, which had caused the instant death of his beloved wife, and their two year old daughter.

After he left the Navy in 1954, Andrew had been able to buy a small semi-detached house on the outskirts of Southampton, not too far away from the ships and the sea which meant so much to him. Both his parents had died by now, and being an only son he had inherited enough money to live very comfortably, when added to his Naval Captains pension. He did not feel any need to go out and get a job, and as he was by nature careful with money, he could devote himself to his two great hobbies, reading and model making.

Both hobbies had been almost life long interests, and were ones he could pursue in the cramped conditions of life aboard ship. His reading tastes were catholic, with fact and fiction mixed in almost equal proportions. But his model making was very specialised, being entirely devoted to ships. Having no home and no family to support for the previous twelve years, Andrew had been able to spend a considerable proportion of his pay on the more challenging and intricate models on the market. He had tried, and discarded, plastic models early on, and most of the models he built now were made of wood, and often built up plank by plank.

In his extensive collection now there were a few sailing ships, but most of his models were tugs or trawlers, corvettes or frigates, and fishing drifters and small coasters. There was a very impressive steam powered paddle steamer, and an equally impressive diesel powered motor torpedo boat, capable of a remarkable turn of speed.

After much searching, Andrew had found a very suitable place to test and sail his growing fleet, about two miles away from his home. He would wait for a fine day, and then load several of his model ships into the back of his small estate car, and drive down to the park. The boating lake was very close to a small car park, which was very convenient. Andrew found there not only tranquil and pleasant surroundings, with a few waterfowl pottering about out in the lake, but also a small number of like minded enthusiasts, who did not attempt to socialise over much, but quietly concentrated like Andrew on enjoying their all consuming hobby.

It was in early 1960 that Andrew decided to embark on his most ambitious project yet. In fact he took the decision on what would have been his wife's forty second birthday. He had spotted a picture in a book on sailing ships of a four masted barque, with what seemed to him the most beautiful lines. Moreover, she was English built, and had been a very fast ship in her day. The rigging would be a great challenge for him, but he felt up to tackling it after having had so many years of experience. And he decided on that special day that his new ship would be called "Catherine" after his dead wife. She would be the most special ship in his whole collection.

Andrew was able to devote a lot of time to his project once he was started on it, and he had the basic hull finished in about two months. It was indeed a delicate and beautiful hull, built up plank by plank, and about three feet long at the waterline. The curved bows, and counter, with bowsprit and mizzen boom added about a further foot.

The masts and main fittings took a further month, together with the rudder, but the sails and rigging were a hard three months slog, even with the help of his faithful sewing machine. Andrew was determined that every detail on his ship should be exactly right. It was early August before the Catherine was fully complete and ready for her maiden voyage.

Andrew picked a perfect Sunday evening, with a gentle breeze that would be blowing across the lake, and keep his ship clear of the island. Andrew was a bit apprehensive about the self steering gear he had devised and fitted himself.

He was glad that when he arrived there were few other people about. There was something very special about this new ship for him, something he had never felt with any of the others. It truly embodied all the grace and beauty he remembered in his long dead wife. The boating lake was partly screened by trees and bushes, but with plenty of open areas on both sides for the launching and retrieving of boats. Most of them brought a long stick with a large hook on the end to help in catching a wayward ship. Andrew had never had to take to the water himself to carry out a rescue, but he had watched fellow boatmen do so on several occasions when their craft had become involved in some kind of disaster, - a suddenly exploding boiler on a tug had been most impressive, and Andrew knew that on average the lake was about three feet deep, or half a fathom.

He spent about an hour rigging his boat, adjusting the sails, and checking the self steering gear. Then he carefully placed her in the water, murmuring "I name this ship Catherine. May God bless her and all who sail in her." It was something he always did at the start of a maiden voyage, though he would never have admitted it to a soul.

Andrew turned the Catherine so that the evening breeze filled her sails, and then gave her a gentle push out into the lake. Immediately he had to begin walking round the side of the lake, so as to reach the far shore before his ship did, and all the time he never took his eyes off her. She was sailing with the wind on her beam, and was pretty close hauled, and she heeled nicely to the gentle wind, and creamed through the water. Her steering gear seemed to be working very well indeed. He watched her critically. She needed to have her trim altered a little, - she was a little high at the bow, but a small alteration in the position of her ballast would soon remedy that. Her jib was not setting quite as well as it should, but never the less she looked utterly beautiful as she sped across the lake in the evening sunshine, and Andrew was secretly thrilled with her.

As he approached the further side of the lake, he was aware that a car had driven noisily into the other car park, but he did not do more than note the fact, as all his concentration was on his wonderful ship. He was waiting for her at the edge of the lake when she sailed in, and caught her gently before she could touch the side. He didn't want even a scratch on her bowsprit. It took him about five minutes to re-adjust the sails, and reset the jib, and then he turned her round, and set her off again on her return voyage across the lake. He felt a great thrill of satisfaction, and utterly at peace with the world.

The Catherine made another excellent passage, even better than the first, but with the onset of the evening Andrew noticed that the breeze was dropping a little. He also noticed that a large man had come down to the edge of the lake the far side, and was fiddling with a model motor boat of considerable size. Andrew felt torn, He longed to do just one more return passage with his new ship, yet he knew that the breeze would continue to drop, and he did not in the least want an audience if his ship became becalmed. When he retrieved the Catherine the second time, he hesitated, not quite sure what to do. But it seemed cruel to take the lovely ship out of her element so quickly, so he re-trimmed the sails, checked the bilge to make sure no water was seeping in, and finding not a drop took that as a good omen, and pushed his ship out again. It was only as he stood up that he got a good look at the man on the bank opposite.

He was a large, stocky, dark and bearded individual. He was dressed in jeans, and an open necked shirt, and on his head he wore a pseudo yachting cap. Round his neck was a strap, which supported a small console of a type Andrew had read about and seen in pictures, but never actually met before. From it sprouted a large radio aerial, and there was an aerial also on the cabin top of the motor boat, disguised not very well as a sort of mast. The motor boat was obviously diesel powered, judging by the noise it was making, and it was the sort which could be purchased for a large sum of money in a high class model shop. It was the sort of outfit Andrew totally despised.

The breeze by now was very light, and the Catherine glided gracefully across the lake for her third crossing. This one would take a lot longer, and in fact Andrew decided that it would have to be the last one after all. He did not want to stay, anyway, for the noisy motor boat was now careering round the lake, shattering the tranquillity, and making a wash that sent waves sloshing over the deck of the Catherine. Andrew walked slowly round the side of the lake again, feeling frustrated and annoyed. His evening, one he had looked forward to for so long, had been spoiled. He was about half way round when he saw the motor boat turn at the far end of the lake, and head straight towards him, and the Catherine. The noise of its motor increased, and its bow rose an inch out of the water as it gathered even more speed. Suddenly Andrew saw that it was heading straight for his slow moving barque, and he shouted and waved his arms.

But he was quite helpless. The crash seemed amazingly loud in the stillness of the evening, despite the noise the motor boat was making. The Catherine was thrown over on her beam ends by the impact, and the motor boat stopped dead, and then went noisily into reverse. As it backed off, the Catherine began to sink, her delicate side completely stove in by the sharp metal bow. Andrew did not hesitate. In a moment he was in the water, and wading towards his ship. He just reached her as her sails began to disappear, and he gently brought her back to the surface. Then he looked up. The man had brought his boat to the bank, and stopped its engine. Now their eyes met.

"What a tragedy" said the man, mockingly, "you see, mate, this one doesn't know about steam giving way to sail" and he gave a nasty laugh, and picked his boat out of the water.

Andrew could never remember afterwards how he got home. He was aware vaguely of loading what was left of his precious ship into the back of his car. Of driving, cold and very wet, along the familiar route. Of taking the Catherine out at home, and gently putting her shattered hull on the cradle he had specially made to hold her. He could not remember what became of the evil man and his stinking motor boat. A veil seemed to have been drawn over most of the events by the lake that evening. Long into the night he sat in his chair and just stared at his Catherine. He felt he must be in a kind of shock once again. He did not even bother to change out of his wet clothes, and eventually dozed in his chair. It was fortunately a mild night, and the house was quite warm.

Around three in the morning he woke suddenly and with a vivid flash of memory. He could vividly see that man, standing on the side of the lake and mocking him and his precious ship. A cold, violent rage suddenly gripped Andrew, something that had not happened to Andrew since the day in 1942 when they told him about his wife and child and his home. His mind began to race, planning, questioning, calculating. By 6.a.m. his plans were complete to the last detail, and his mind was made up. Now speed was essential, and he set to work at once.

He first spent a busy hour measuring the compact battery on the lawn mower, looking out the electric motor which had come off the fan of his old Austin A.35 that had eventually and sadly gone to the scrapyard, and finding other motors and switches in his workshop. Then to the drawing board, and lots of calculations to be done. By 9.30.a.m. he was down at the Princedale Engineering Works, talking to his friend Clive, who had done a variety of small jobs for him in the past.

"She'll have to be pretty big to carry all that weight, Andrew," said Clive, peering at his drawings and figures through thick spectacles.

"That doesn't matter", replied Andrew, "as long as I can lift her in and out of the water. I wondered about using aluminium?"

"Good idea for the weight, but it's expensive."

"Have you got any suitable sheets?"

"Yes" said Clive, and they made their way to the back of the large workshop, and began looking some out.

"I'll leave it with you" said Andrew eventually. "Don't worry about the cost, but please put that reinforcement in the bow exactly as I've sketched it in. And I would be most grateful if it could be done as soon as possible."

"You're in luck" said Clive. "August is always a quiet month, and I reckon I can get it done in a week or less. Andrew returned home, with a feeling of quiet satisfaction. For the next few days he made careful and detailed plans and drawings, and worked on various fittings in his workshop. Whenever he had finished work, he covered over his project with an old sheet. He only ventured out once, to collect a book on radio controlled models which he had ordered from a local bookshop. He spent several hours each evening mastering the new technical knowledge which he needed to understand. On the Friday Clive rang him, and he drove straight down to collect the four foot long aluminium hull which had been made for him. It just fitted neatly into the back of his estate car, with the seat down, just as he had intended it should. Also, he was very pleased that it was not as heavy as he feared it would be.

For the next few weeks Andrew worked almost night and day on his ship. Try as he might, he could not break the habit of a lifetime, and sacrifice quality for speed. Only on a Sunday evening did he stop work early, and drive down to the boating lake. He no longer parked in the car park, but in the small road nearby, and then he walked to a concealed vantage point where he could stand and watch what was happening. He wore an old hat and sun glasses, and carried his binoculars with him.

On three of the four Sunday evenings the pirate with the motor boat came down to the lake, and at almost exactly the same time. He proceeded to shatter the peace of the area every time, and to terrorise any other boating enthusiasts who might still be there. In fact most people cleared off the moment they saw him coming, and in a very few minutes he had the lake to himself, which was just what he wanted. Andrew's hatred matured week by week.

At the end of the first week in September Andrew's ship was ready. She was obviously a naval warship, rather on the lines of an old fashioned destroyer, with a single gun mounted forward, and two quite high funnels. She was a little too broad in the beam, but that enabled her to house the mower battery amidships, fixed to her bottom and providing the main part of her ballast. The battery could be charged up by connecting his trickle charger to a small concealed plug on her deck. The electric motor was connected via a shaft to a single screw, made of brass. Fortunately, Andrew had already had this in stock, so was not obliged to make it from scratch.

Andrew built an open bridge, radio aerials and other fittings. As usual, all was perfectly to scale, except the single gun on the forward deck, which posed some special problems and took a good deal of time. He also had to build in the radio receiver, which was a new experience, and connect up the steering motor and the throttle rheostat. Finally, she was painted the regulation grey, and her deck was carefully varnished. She looked very smart, and a little menacing.

On the following Sunday evening Andrew was early at the lake, parked in the car park, and had his new ship in the water for trials within a few minutes. It was fortunate that he was a fit man, as carrying her to put her in the water, and floating her, took a lot of strength. The sea trials were a great success. A few adjustments needed to be made, one to the elevation adjustment of the gun, after Andrew had carefully measured the height of the water. Then, having checked that he was now on his own, he slipped off his shoes and socks, and took off his trousers to reveal a pair of shorts underneath. These he put in his car, before parking it out of sight. He then climbed into the water, which was very fresh, to say the least, and carefully pushed his boat out to the island. Here he held her in place, using two sticks driven into the muddy bottom, and then he pulled a branch off a small tree nearby, and used it to cover the ship so that it was difficult to see her, but she could yet emerge easily from underneath. Unless someone actually came round the back of the island, it was very unlikely she would be spotted.

Andrew stood in the slightly murky water and looked at her with pride. Her name, "Vengeance," in gold lettering, gleamed on her bow. Andrew waded back to the shore, dried himself, and put his trousers, socks and shoes on again. Then he got into his car, checked he had a good view of the lake, and waited.

Suddenly, only ten minutes later, the by now familiar car roared into the car park on the opposite side. Andrew felt his scalp tingle as he saw the man get out. Tonight he was wearing a windcheater and a red woolly hat to guard against the cold, and for a moment he stood looking at the empty lake with a satisfied grin. Then he opened the boot of his car, and lifted out his boat as usual. Andrew watched as he placed it in the water, switched on the motor, and then put on the radio control console strapped to his shoulders. He moved the throttle lever, spun the wheel, and the boat started its noisy and familiar voyage round the lake. Andrew gently opened his car door, and raised the aerial on his own console. Then he eased his throttle forward, and watched the island shore in apprehension. With an almost audible sigh of relief he saw "Vengeance" gliding out, clear of the sticks and the branch. Now he must judge his moment to perfection. He watched the motor boat. It was moving down the lake at full speed, away from him. Soon it would have to turn and retrace its course, as he had seen it do so often. He picked a point on the lake in his minds eye, and judged the distance between the two boats, and the necessary speed. The motor boat swung round at the end of the lake, and came churning back. Andrew moved his throttle further open, and in total silence "Vengeance" picked up speed. He moved his miniature wheel, and she altered course a couple of points to port. Up to that point the other man had been quite unaware of any other ship on the lake, but now the movement must have caught his eye. He instinctively altered course to head for Andrews boat, unable to see all that clearly as he was facing the sunset, and the light was beginning to fade.

For a few seconds the two craft headed straight towards one another. Andrew increased speed to full ahead. Suddenly, in the poorer light, the other man became aware of the size of his adversary. He must have swung his steering wheel, for his boat began a sharp turn. But Andrew had anticipated him, and "Vengeance" also turned a little, so that when the collision came she struck the motor boat full amidships, and with her weight and momentum completely overrode it, so that it disappeared beneath her strengthened bow, never to reappear.

Andrew looked up. The hairy man was standing on the edge of the lake, his mouth open, twiddling the knobs on his radio console in an almost hypnotised state. Andrew moved his wheel, and eased back on his throttle. This remote control business was rather fun, after all. He smiled. Now "Vengeance" was heading straight for the man on the opposite bank, watched with total concentration by the men on opposite sides of the lake. Andrew screwed up his eyes in the poor light, and then suddenly his finger pushed down on the red knob on his control panel.

Across the lake a shot rang out, and two ducks on the water near the island took to the wing with quacks of alarm. A moorhen scuttered in under the bank. From the gun on the vengeance a slight curl of smoke drifted away across the surface. But Andrew was watching the man on the bank, even as his fingers moved the wheel and "Vengeance" began a gentle turn.

The man stood stock still for a second or two, and then he lifted his arms above his shoulders, slowly, and pitched forward into the lake, console and all. The weight of the console took him beneath the water at once, and soon the ripples died away across the lake, leaving a perfectly tranquil scene. Only a red woolly hat floated soggily on the surface to buoy the spot.

Andrew brought the "Vengeance" safely back to the side of the lake, and switched off her motor. He drove his car over, and with some difficulty lifted her out and installed her on the cradle he had made for her. Then for several minutes he stood looking out over the nearly dark lake. The moorhen had come out again and was slowly crossing the water. He felt a deep sense of peace. Then he climbed into his car, and drove gently home in the darkness. He would have a celebration supper, an omelette and a glass or two of wine.

In the days that followed Andrew decided to repair the "Catherine." He worked slowly and very patiently taking the hull to pieces, and shaping the new planks necessary to replace those that had been shattered. It was quite a mammoth task, but he was actually very glad to have a project to keep his mind occupied, for it was a time of waiting. He spent a good deal of time looking at "Vengeance" on her cradle in the hall, and wondering whether to dismantle the gun? But how would he fill the obvious gap that would be left? And he was proud of that gun, with its solenoid triggered spring firing mechanism, and its .22 bore barrel that he had adapted to take a single cartridge. He decided to leave it, but he did remove the red knob from the console, and replaced it with a black one labelled "Hooter." It never actually functioned.

In was six days later. On the Saturday afternoon, that the front door bell rang. There had been quite a lot about the mystery in the local paper, of course. There had been some discussion on the local radio, and even pictures of police frogmen in the lake on local television. It had, as usual, all blown over in a couple of days.

The policeman on the front doorstep was a kindly looking man, in later middle age.

"I'm so sorry to be disturbing you on a Saturday afternoon," he said. "I do hope you weren't watching the football, sir."

Andrew assured him that was not the case, and invited him in. In the living room the policeman said

"We are just making a few enquiries about that business down at the boating lake in the park last week. Would I be right in thinking that you have an interest in model ships?"

Then his gaze fell on the rows of beautiful models all round the room, and the question didn't really need an answer. Soon they were talking ships, and it transpired that the policeman had also been in the Royal Navy, for a three year short service period. Presently the policeman gratefully accepted a cup of tea, and was then reminded of the actual purpose of his visit. It was in connection with the man who had been shot down at the boating lake some time last Sunday night.

"I don't suppose you happened to see anything down there that day that might help us, sir?"

Andrew shook his head, and said that regretfully he could not help.

"You don't yourself possess any firearm?" asked the policeman, a little apologetically, sipping his tea.

"No, and never have" said Andrew, "but you are very welcome to look round the house if you feel you should."

"No, no" said the policeman, hastily. "I really don't think that's at all necessary. Anyway," he added, dropping his voice a little, "I'm not so sure about all this shooting business. Between you and me the forensic people are arguing like hell between themselves about what they think they found. They actually believe, some of them, that the shot was fired from well below the chap, and then he fell forward into the water. They make it sound as though someone surfaced from the bottom of the pond and took a shot at him. Quite ridiculous, I think, when you put it like that." He finished his tea, and the conversation soon returned to the subject of model boats. They made a general tour of inspection of Andrew's fleet together, and then the policeman regretfully announced that he must be on his way after a very pleasant and interesting visit.

On his way to the front door the policeman spotted "Vengeance" and ran a critical eye over her. He seemed a little worried about something to do with the forward gun, the scale perhaps. But all he said was "My God, I wish I could make a ship the way you do, sir."

Then he opened the front door, and with a cheery goodbye and a wave of his hand, passed out of Andrew's life.

TWELVE.   THE CAT.

It began, as so many things do, with a telephone call out of the blue. It was lunchtime, and Peter, well and truly retired, was cooking himself a boiled egg. His wife still worked, and he was fond of saying that he sent her out to earn their living.

"Is that Mr Fosset" asked a woman's voice, a little hesitantly.

"How can I help you?" Peter replied, automatically.

"I got your name because you wrote an article on jigsaw puzzles for Saga Magazine a couple of years ago, and I kept the article because I knew we had this old wooden puzzle up in the loft somewhere, and I wanted to know a bit more about it, and whether someone would like it."

Peter's heart sank somewhat. It was invariably an old Victory children's puzzle, with four pieces missing, picture of a thatched cottage or two cows, and the family dog had chewed the box. It was sometimes difficult to explain to people that their cherished treasure, even if fifty years old, was not even worth taking to a Charity Shop.

"I'll certainly help if I can" said Peter. "Does your puzzle have a box with it?"

"Yes" said the caller.

"Is there a makers name on the box?" asked Peter.

"It says it is made by V.T.H. Puzzles."

"I'm afraid I've never heard of them" said Peter.

"They called themselves the Maids of Kent Craft Shop" supplemented the caller.

A small bell began to ring for Peter. Where had he come across that name before? The Maids of Kent, and a Wooden Puzzle. It seemed to link with a fabulous puzzle which was depicted on the cover of his main Jigsaw Puzzle reference book. The picture was of Alice in Wonderland, with the Mock Turtle and the Gryphon either side of her. It was very striking indeed. The Maids of Kent he seemed to remember kept a craft shop, and they ran a library lending out wooden jigsaw puzzles. They were called Helen Helmore and Vera Tassell, and they cut their own puzzles with incredible skill and fiendish cunning!

"What size is your old puzzle?" asked Peter. His hand, holding the telephone, shook a little.

"It measures about twenty nine inches by twenty one inches, and has just under nine hundred pieces" replied the caller.

Peter's voice was threatening to let him down, as his excitement mounted. It sounded just the size he would have expected.

"What is the subject of the picture on the puzzle?" he asked.

"It's Alice in Wonderland" replied the caller.

It can't be a duplicate, thought Peter. Trying to keep his voice steady, he said

"What is Alice doing?"

"She's talking to the Cheshire Cat" was the reply.

Peter did not quite know what to say. It was as though his spade had turned over a large clod of earth and there was the glint of gold beneath. The puzzle on the book cover was not unique then. It had a twin. Perhaps there were a set. A mad hatter's tea party, croquet game, court scene, gardeners painting roses. He was brought back to earth by the lady asking whether he thought the puzzle had any value. It was complete, and in good condition.

Peter thought quickly. It was unfair to take advantage of her ignorance of jigsaw puzzle values, but when he named a three-figure sum, he heard a sharp intake of breath. Feeling a little light-headed, almost reckless in his excitement, he added the cost of postage as well, and asked if the puzzle could be sent as soon as convenient.

To Peter's surprise and joy it arrived two days later. He kept his side of the bargain, and sent off the cheque as soon as he had inspected the puzzle to see all was well. The condition of puzzle and box was even better than he had dared hope for. And the small photograph filled him with excitement, for Alice was dressed in exactly the same clothes as in the other picture, - in fact it was undoubtedly the same Alice by the same artist, though he could not read the signature. Peter wrapped the parcel again, tied it up with string, and placed it reverently in a corner of the room by his bed, where he could gloat over it until he opened it again on Christmas Day.

In the days which followed Peter watched over his treasure, occasionally picking it up to inspect when his wife was not around. He phoned several jigsaw puzzle friends, and had a quiet and most satisfactory gloat. He imagined the moment when he would unwrap it again, pour out the torrent of pieces. He planned the setting, the time of day.

Christmas Day came at last, and Peter kept his present until the evening, almost as though he was afraid to open it. Finally the moment came. The brown box was even better and more impressive than he had remembered. The condition of the pieces in their cloth bag with the embroidered initials on it was even better than he had hoped. The small photograph gave a glimpse of the majesty of the full picture, with Alice standing in the foreground, and the cat up on the lowest branch of the tree, it's yellow eyes staring intently.

Peter spent a couple of hours quietly sorting the pieces, while some of his favourite music played in the background. He had even planned the appropriate Beethoven for the occasion. Then, suddenly feeling unaccountably tired, he had a final Christmas night cap, and went off to bed.

The following day was surprisingly busy, with drinks with friends at noon which as usual went on and on, so that they did not get home until it was almost dark. Later in the evening Peter tackled the puzzle again, and assembly began in earnest. He did the sky, which was relatively easy and not a large patch. He then tackled Alice herself, and she too was distinctive and fairly easy, though where she joined the tree was tricky. It was getting late, but he determined to finish the cat also. The head was not hard, and the large greenish yellow eyes almost seemed to find themselves. But the colours on the animals back were much harder and merged into colours of leaves and dried grass, so that when he finally decided to give up and go to bed, two pieces of the cat's back were still missing. Its eyes seemed to look at him reproachfully as he got up to leave the room.

The next day was wet, dark and dismal, and his wife was back at work. Peter decided to have a long session at his puzzle. He did his morning chores, got an extra lamp, and settled down to work as soon as he was able. Now the puzzle was far harder, with the subtle greens and browns of tree branches and leaves, grass and path very hard to disentangle. Further, to make the task much harder, the puzzle had been line cut, so that the cut line separated one colour from another, and you never knew what colour the next piece would be. Frequently he found a piece he spent ages hunting for was not at all as he had imagined it would be. He could almost hear the two Maids of Kent chuckling at his frustration. And every time he moved round his puzzle table to tackle a different section of the picture, he found the cat's eyes followed him, and stared at him in a disconcerting manner. He even contemplated putting something over the cat's head, and then dismissed the thought as ridiculous.

He also found that even with a good light his eyes seemed to tire quickly, and he had to take short breaks to rest them. With that factor, and a few other distractions like food and walking the dog, progress was singularly slow, and by the time his wife returned the puzzle was less than half done, and a lot of household chores had been neglected. Peter's wife was not pleased with him.

Peter did not sleep well. He kept thinking about the puzzle, wanting to be tackling it again, yet in some strange way repelled by it. He tried to analyse what it was about the puzzle that affected him so much, and couldn't. And when he closed his eyes, he seemed to see the eyes of the cat glowing in the dark above him.

He awoke with a steely determination to finish the puzzle however long it took him. He told his wife of his resolution at breakfast, and received a very noticeable lack of support. He rushed through the essential jobs, and settled down to the puzzle. Once again he felt himself engaged in a conflict, and every piece seemed to be a struggle. Time and again he thought he had found a piece, only to discover he had been slightly mistaken about the shape, or the colour, and it would not fit. By lunchtime progress was still very slow. The afternoon seemed to fly by, and still huge gaps in the picture remained, mainly the foliage of the trees, and the area of grass. Grudgingly he left the puzzle and prepared things for supper, and did the washing up. His wife arrived home late, and there was a stand-off because Peter had promised to walk the vacuum cleaner round the house, and completely forgotten to do so. It was nearly 9.p.m. when he settled down to the puzzle again, determined to finish it in one sitting. His wife bade him a curt goodnight, made some sotto voce comment about puzzles and those who stayed up all night doing them, and went off to bed.

Peter adjusted his two lights, and settled down to defeat the puzzle once and for all.

The lights cast a pool of brilliance in the otherwise darkened room. Outside, he could hear the wind was getting up. It took him at least ten minutes to fit the first piece, and frustration started to build up. Interwoven with the sound of the wind he sometimes felt he could hear the undulating sound of a machine, rather like the sound of an old fashioned sewing machine, but with a rasp to it as well. A picture of an old lady bent over a treadle saw came to mind. She was smiling, a rather machiavellian smile. Peter redoubled his efforts, but he could not even sort the pieces into shapes or patterns because they were so varied and complex.

Presently he noticed something a little strange about the cat's tail, where it hung down below the tree branch. The end of it seemed rather fuzzy and indistinct. Peter assumed some dust from somewhere had settled on it, and wiped his finger across it. The tail remained faded, and when he looked at his finger, there was no sign of dust or paint on it. And if anything the tail seemed even more indistinct. It must be his eyes, or a trick of the light. He moved one of the lights a little, and set to work on a different piece of tree foliage. He avoided looking at the cat's tail.

"….This time the cat vanished quite slowly, beginning with the end of the tail, and ending with the grin, which remained some time after the rest of it had gone." The words from the classic suddenly came into his mind, though it must be years since he had read them. He stole a look at the cat. The tail was hard to make out, and surely the cat's rear end was looking a little less distinct now? A sudden fear came over Peter. He had to finish the puzzle, before the cat vanished. He could not tell why, but his very life depended on it. With a sort of frenzy he started trying every piece in every available space. Method and plan were thrown to the winds, time was all that mattered.

The wind outside howled in the chimney. Peter stared at the rear end of the cat. Its tail had completely disappeared, and been replaced by tree foliage. Its back was fading, almost as he watched. He felt the hairs on the back of his neck stir. It must be a trick of the light, or was he going mad? He re-doubled his efforts, and quite quickly put four more pieces in place. The grass beside the path was just about completed. In spite of himself he raised his eyes, and looked at the cat on the branch above. Only the front half now remained, and the eyes glowed balefully, looking straight back at him.

longer could they encourage one another with talk of "The Nelson touch." When the remnants of the Franco-Spanish fleet disengaged at nightfall, the "Royal Sovereign" with her Admiral, now Commander-in –Chief in Nelsons place, was among the ships which escorted the badly mauled "Victory" down to the sheltered harbour at Gibralter. Once the ships carpenter and his mates had attended to the plugging of shot holes, of which there were a goodly number, he was able to find time to do a temporary repair on the Admirals dining table. It would have to do for the present, - in fact it worked very well for the next 135 years!

Admiral of the Fleet Lord Collingwood continued his distinguished service in the Royal Navy until his sad death at sea in March 1810. He was then in command of the "Ville de Paris" and his table had followed him on each ship he had commanded. In due course the table served his successor, a much less distinguished Rear Admiral, but there were no more battles. Britain's total supremacy at sea was unchallenged for over 100 years, apart from the odd action by some cheeky colonists across the Atlantic, and the table never had to double as an operating table again. Admirals and captains would sit round it passing the Port, and spinning yarns about deeds of daring in past years. But sadly, as the 19th Century progressed, the old wooden warships became obsolete, and were broken up. One of the South Coast ports where this dismantling was carried out was Dartmouth, and it was to this port that the old "Invincible" was sailed, in the year 1846, to be decommissioned and either broken up, or taken up river to join two prison hulks which the Navy already maintained there. In the event, the latter course of action was decided upon, and once the proud ship had been hulked, she was taken up to Dartmouth Creek and moored alongside the other hulks. Captain Rumbelow, who was the rather aptly named Commanding Officer of the hulks, inspected his new ship, and being impressed with the commanding officers accommodation, transferred his flag to the "Invincible," and set about making good and very regular use of the dining table.

In due course a fourth hulk was added, the poor old "Resolution", and conditions in the four ships grew steadily worse as their captain spent more and more time sampling vintage wines in his dining cabin, and less and less time overseeing the conditions on the ships under his command. A good officer would have detected that the mood of the prisoners was not just sullen and uncooperative, but getting near to the point of mutiny. Sadly Captain Horace Rumbelow, now thoroughly disillusioned and bitter at his lack of further promotion, and the dead end job to which he had been assigned, was not a good officer.

The mutiny, when it came, was, as so often is the case, sparked off by a seemingly trivial incident. A prisoner, - one of the more assertive characters of the prisoners on board "Invincible" disobeyed a command given to him by a bullying Petty Officer. The Petty Officer struck the prisoner with his cane, whereupon the prisoner struck the Petty Officer, and when he fell to the deck, seized his cutlass and dealt him a blow which was instantly fatal. The crews on all the hulks had never been up to strength, and the mutineers fought with a dogged desperation, using any weapons they could lay their hands on. Fortunately for the authorities the mutiny lacked any planning or direction, and on the other three ships the prisoners were all locked in their cells at that time of day. Only the men up on deck for 'exercise' on "Invincible" could join in. They were soon surrounded, and retreated down the aft companionway, which was the only means of escape. This led to the Captain's quarters, and they burst into the Captains Day cabin. Captain Rumbelow had heard some noise outside and above on deck, but being in a fairly stupefied state had not taken a lot of notice of it. He was taken completely by surprise, and though he did manage to fire off a pistol with hopeless inaccuracy, he was cut down with the same cutlass which had recently dispatched the hapless Petty Officer.

The dozen or so mutineers then proceeded to barricade themselves in the cabin, using the dining table, on its side, to barricade the door. Its spare leaves were piled against it, and then two men, one with an axe, chopped up the cabinet which held the leaves and the pieces were used to wedge the table in place. The mutineers then waited to see what the next move of the crew would be. They were so busy watching the door, and listening for sounds that would give them a clue, that they never saw two boats from the other hulks, full of sailors and marines, creep into view through the large stern window. The first they knew of the danger was a ragged volley of musket shots, and the collapse of five of their number onto the deck. Three of the mutineers ran to the shattered window, but they just presented easier targets for the marines. In half a minute the mutiny was over, the mutineers left alive surrendering at once.

The aftermath to this bloody affair came in two parts. One resulted in stiff bodies hanging from the yardarms of any nearby ships still equipped with them. The Navy would never tolerate mutiny in any form, and the hanging corpses were a grim warning "pour encourager les autres." The second part consisted in the writing of the inevitable report for the Lords Commissioners of the Admiralty.

The lot fell to Rear Admiral John Duckworth, Officer commanding the Dartmouth Training Squadron, to attend to this tedious duty. The crew of "Invincible" had done their best to tidy up after the lurid happenings on board their ship, and when the Rear Admiral inspected the late Captains Cabins, the blood stains had been cleaned off the floor. He spent some time looking round and taking notes, for it was here that the greatest crime of all had been committed, the slaying of a Commanding

Officer on board his own ship. He noted the furniture in the cabin. The cabinet, or what was left of it, had been put out for fuel for the galley fire. The table had been restored to its rightful position, with its spare leaves stacked against the wall. Admiral Duckworth looked at the table long and hard, and liked what he saw.

The First Lieutenant remarked "It is said, sir, that it belonged to Admiral Collingwood, and was at the battle of Trafalgar."

The Admiral grunted, but he made a mental note. In a few months he would be hoisting his flag in "Britannia" which was to be anchored in Dartmouth Harbour as the first Naval Cadet training ship. He would be needing to do quite a lot of entertaining, he guessed. He was quite right, for the Navy was building up its strength once again, as the demands of a great and expanding Empire were placed upon it. The cadet training ship, "Britannia" was now assisted by several other smaller craft, and Dartmouth harbour was always full of small cutters and whalers doing sailing and rowing drills. Senior Naval officers from London and other parts of the country were always turning up to "see how things were going" and they all expected hospitality at the Admirals table.

For the next 36 years, as Britain developed her navy, and new and more powerful ships emerged from the shipyards, Dartmouth and its Training Squadron became ever more important, and the table supported many an important dinner, and listened to endless deep discussions by seafaring folk on the latest techniques and tactics. Finally, in 1905 it was decided that a change must be made. Not only was the old "Britannia" beginning to show her considerable age, but the whole Naval training programme was so vast that a shore based College seemed the only way of accommodating all the cadets in training, and doing so with efficiency. Thus, on the hill overlooking Dartmouth harbour on the western side, the Royal Naval College was built, and it has served the navy ever since.

But what about the table? The Admiral in command in 1905 gave directions that it was to be transferred to the shore based college, along with all his other furniture. For a number of years, - we cannot be certain exactly how many, it continued to serve as his dining table, in the new dining room at the college. However, it became gradually apparent that it was not large enough for its increasing customers, and the dining room could accommodate a table twice the size. So it was first moved into the anteroom, and reduced in size, and a new splendid table was made for the Admirals dining room. No one knew the history of the old table, and in those hectic times before the first world war it is doubtful if anyone would have been very interested.

After the war the college in Dartmouth continued with its vital work, but after a time the ante-room was refurnished, and the table was moved to a storeroom down in the basement. There it remained, dusty and largely forgotten, until the mid 1930s.

By 1935 the Britannia Royal Naval College was becoming ever more busy, as the Navy once again built up its strength, and storm clouds began to gather over Europe. A new Admiral arrived to preside over the college, and he was full of energy and given much to efficiency, which was just what the college required. On his initial inspection he even found his way down into the basement, and a rather flustered officer was called upon to give an account of what he found there. The Admiral decreed that it was high time the basement was cleared out, - there was abundant evidence of the presence of rats who had been leading a very comfortable life with no need to ever abandon sinking ships!

Anything that was saleable was to be sold, and the money could be put in the Officers Mess Wine fund. The rest was to be taken out to the back yard and burnt when the wind was favourable. The Admiral moved on to other duties.

There was a short debate about the table, as it was noticed that it was damaged. However, it seemed in reasonable condition, and so it was put with the things that Mr. Atwill, a second hand furniture dealer with a shop down in the town, was due to come and look at with a view to making an offer for them. In due course Mr. Atwill arrived, and made an offer for the lot. Mentally he valued the table at about £2, having gloomily pointed out the damaged leg and frame. Before the week was out it was tucked away, with its spare leaves, at the back of his shop. He always had a few nice pieces of furniture in the window, to tempt people to come in.

In the summer of 1935, Captain Oliver Tyler had bought a "charming gentleman's residence" in the village of Broadhempston, and he needed to furnish its three reception and six bedrooms. One day, on his way back from a visit to his brother at East Portlemouth, beside the Salcombe Estuary, he remembered that his brother had mentioned a good little second hand furniture shop in Dartmouth. He decided that a detour would be in order, and after a couple of enquiries he found Mr Atwill's shop tucked away in a back street a few yards from the harbour. Oliver Tyler went in, activating the old metal bell that hung above the door, and was beginning to look round, not very hopefully, when the proprietor popped in from the back yard, where he was "restoring" a piece of furniture that had seen much better days.

After some conversation, and Oliver's disinterest in most of what Mr Atwill had to offer, the subject of a dining table came up.

"Ah!" said Mr Atwill, with growing confidence, "now you did zay, zur, as how you've got a big and growing vamily, bain't yeu? Now I've got the verry thing for you , zur, jus 'ere in ther back o the shop."

Mr. Atwill set to work like a dog digging up a bone, and wishing it was not such a hot day. After a few minutes most of the table was revealed.

"Ther t'is" Mr. Atwill declared triumphantly. "You won't find anuther loverly table like that for hundred miles, zur."

Captain Tyler got down on his hands and knees and looked underneath. It certainly was a curious table, with its cantilever frame and its ten legs. He took careful note of the damage.

"Have you got the extra leaves that fit into it?"

"Over ere, zur," said Mr Atwill, proudly, "all four of them be ere, good as new."

"I'm sorry to see the frame is so badly damaged," said the Captain.

"Ah, that's naught, zur" responded Mr Atwill, a little too quickly. "I jus aven't got round to it yet, but twill take jus a couple of minutes to put en right" he added with unfounded optimism. He unfortunately couldn't know that the Captain was a very good carpenter and engineer.

Captain Tyler stood and looked at the table. "How much?" he asked. Truth to tell, he was getting a little tired of Mr. Atwill.

Mr Atwill stood and considered. The table was certainly quite badly damaged, and its size would not appeal to very many people. He had picked it up for a song, moreover, even in these depressed times. And he needed the cash, quite badly.

"I'd be cheating meeself if I let un go for less that ten pound," he declared.

Oliver Tyler picked up his hat, and made to leave. "I could drop it to eight, mebbee" said Mr Atwill, in some desperation. Eventually they settled on five pounds, and an extra two to have it delivered the following week to Broadhempston, when the lorry did its weekly rounds.

When the table arrived at Elm Park, Oliver had it put in the large garage which also served as his woodworking shop. He laid an old blanket on the long bench, and with the aid of his newly acquired gardener, Frank, laid the table bottom up on the surface. When he had a moment to spare, and life was exceedingly busy, he had a good look at the table.

A repair would be fairly easy, and he had some suitable wood which he had brought back from Kenya, where he had been a settler for fifteen years. Three struts would make the table strong and rigid once again, but the two end legs would then no longer fold back. The table, at its smallest, would be twice the size it was originally designed to be. This did not worry Oliver as he had a large dining room, and lots of people of all ages to occupy the places round the table. The table was duly installed, given a good coat of polish, and indeed looked very handsome and in keeping with the Georgian style room.

Then began what was a halcyon period for the table. There were always plenty of people, young and old, occupying the chairs round its polished top, and usually two extra leaves at least were required. Food was plentiful, and numbers varied according as to whether it was holiday or term time. There were always one or two black Labrador dogs in residence underneath, waiting hopefully for anything that fell onto the floor. The outbreak of the Second World War did not make a huge difference. Food in a country village was still quite plentiful if you had gardens and orchards, and kept chickens and ducks. When the war was over, numbers in the household continued to rise, there being now nine children, and it was not unusual to sit down 15 to 20 round the Admirals table.

One day, when there was a school half term, Oliver Tyler took his two elder daughters out of school, and for an outing they drove down to Portsmouth. He had long wanted to see over Nelsons Flagship, "H.M.S. Victory" now restored and permanently in dry dock there. The ship was very impressive, and they walked the decks and marvelled at the fittings and guns, but when they came to Nelsons dining cabin they had a great surprise. There, laid ready for a meal, with gleaming silver and glass, was their own dining table, or at least its twin! Every detail was exactly the same, except there was no repair. Also, the cabinet to store the spare leaves was intact, and stood beside the wall of the cabin.

Oliver now realised immediately the significance of his own table, and was in a fair way to guessing its fascinating history.

Oliver died suddenly in 1957, but his widow Grace continued to use the table regularly, even though her large family were scattered. Soon a new generation would be occupying places where Collingwood's officers had sat in times past. When Grace Tyler moved to a smaller house in Devon, and then to Somerset and Sussex, the beautiful table moved with her. But finally there was no room for it in her next bungalow, and she passed it on to her eldest son. At that point there was an attempt to sell the table, but no-one bid as high as the reserve, and it remained in the family.

Now the table has moved to Suffolk, and is in regular use, with dinner parties of up to 18 people. On a winter's evening, lit by the light of many candles, it does not need a great imagination to see it in Collingwood's day, though it does not have to be secured to the floor despite rather severe problems of "Ground Heave" in our bungalow! The table has witnessed over two hundred years of truly momentous history, and it is such a pity it cannot tell it's story for itself.

FOURTEEN. HIGHLAND HOSPITALITY.

William Archer and Timothy Frazer-Halliday met at University
where both were members of the University Rambling Club.
They were always called Bill and Tim by their friends, so we
shall refer to them as such in this account of their particular
activity.

Bill was the taller of the two, and would have done well
playing rugby or rowing in one of the eights. He was over six
feet tall, with a rosy face and a mop of blond hair, which he
allowed to grow to shoulder length on occasions when he
couldn't be bothered to find a barber. One instinctively felt that
somewhere far back in his ancestry there must have been a
Viking chief with a great talent for fraternisation! He had a
strong, mellow voice, and liked to dress casually at all times.

Tim was smaller in every way, but he was strong and wiry,
with a passion for keeping fit. He had a pleasant if slightly
sallow face, brown eyes which derived from his mother, and
dark hair always cut fairly short. Unlike Bill he always looked
smart, even when out Rambling, but he never minded getting
mud on his clothing if it was due to the conditions on a good
ramble.

"Good clean mud will always wash out" was a favourite
saying of his.

Both men lived in London, though at opposite sides of the
metropolis. Bill and his family were down the Thames at
Greenwich, while Tim and his parents,- he was an only son,
lived out at Chiswick. Both men were fortunate in that their
fathers ran their own reasonably prosperous businesses, and so
they did not have to worry about money matters, Both worked
in the family business during vacations, and both expected to
continue to do so on leaving University.

It was towards the end of their last term at university, when
final exams were safely over, that a chance remark in the pub

174

one evening launched a whole new idea. Tim had bought the first pints, and returned to Bill, who was sitting looking rather morose.

Tim said "Ramble on Sunday afternoon. Are you up for it?"

Bill took a good swig of his beer, thought a minute, and asked "Where is it this time?"

"North Downs, somewhere west of Badgers Mount. Lovely views to the south."

Bill grunted. "All within earshot of the beastly M 25" he muttered. "And a considerable coach journey to get there and back."

There was silence for some minutes, as both attended to their drinks.

Bill looked up. "I'm sorry," he said. "I'm not at all good company. End-of-term-itis or something, I suppose. Fact is I've gone off the twee rambles, with all the gossiping and jolly laughter, and the nicely manicured footpaths along England's green and pleasant land. I want to do something challenging, where there are real hills and you need a compass because there aren't little footpath signs every hundred yards."

There was another period of silence, with gentle slurping of beers.

"It's very odd you should say that," said Tim, "because that is exactly what I have been feeling myself. What do you suggest we do?"

Bill's face lit up. "Tomorrow night, Friday, we board the overnight sleeper to Inverness. Get out at Aviemore. Find a small, comfortable hotel, - it's not the skiing season so there are bound to be beds. Walk in the Cairngorms Saturday and Sunday, and get the sleeper back overnight to get us in here some time Monday morning, in time for all those lectures we no longer have to go to!"

"What a brilliant idea "responded Tim. "I can see it now, bracing mountain walk with a wee Highland lassie serving Malt Whisky and Haggis at the end of it!"

"I shall look after the wee Highland lassie," said Bill with a grin.

So began a whole new period in their lives. They both joined their family businesses, and both discovered what the pressures were like in the real world beyond the encircling walls of a cosy university. But they always had the next Highland outing to look forward to. They held planning meetings, with large scale maps, but for some reason they always returned to their base at Aviemore. It was so convenient for the overnight sleeper, and the little hotel was so welcoming and comfortable, even if the wee lassie did not materialise. The malt whisky and excellent haggis made up for her absence, and they often drank a toast to her. They always shared a twin bedded room, for company, but they behaved with true British propriety, and took it in turns to use the bathroom. In fact both had a succession of very attractive girl friends back in London, who were never told of the Highland adventures in case they had demanded to join the next expedition. Both Bill and Tim invented fictitious Aunties who had to be visited to account for their regular absence.

So a number of years went by, until both men were in their mid twenties, unmarried, affluent, and much sought after. They carried big responsibilities in the companies of which they were senior partners, they were under a lot of pressure at work, and the Highland Rambles, as they referred to them, were a source of real relaxation, and of an ever deepening friendship of the true kind.

Christmas 2008 was a very busy time in both businesses, and was not helped by an outbreak of 'flu among both staffs. Bill and Tim both viewed Christmas as an endurance test, and both looked longingly at a circle drawn round four days in mid-

Fifteen Love

January 2009 when they would do a Highland Ramble, and nothing that the world could throw at them would stop the expedition. Somehow, amid the last minute Christmas preparations and the New Year celebrations they managed to get together and hold a couple of planning meetings in their favourite pub.

"What do we do if the weather is perfectly foul?" asked Tim at the second meeting. It was already very cold and producing what in London passes for snow.

"We press on regardless" said Bill, with a look of grim determination. "If the train isn't running we shall have to drive up there."

Tim sipped his beer and tried to visualise the scene. Both drove powerful and luxurious cars, but highland snowdrifts are no respecters of persons.

In the event the snow abated, and though the weather forecast for the Cairngorms was not good, to say the least, the trains were running. Some delays could be expected, they were told, as they boarded the night sleeper at Euston, and prepared to get some much needed sleep.

It was still dark in Aviemore when they clambered out of the train, but in spite of a stiff breeze the sky was clear, with bright stars. Early breakfast was waiting for them in the hotel, with porridge, eggs and bacon, oatcakes and scalding coffee, so that the sight of the sky clouding over, and even an occasional snowflake made the snug room with it's open fire seem more attractive than ever.

"Come on" said Bill, getting to his feet reluctantly. "Now we've got to walk it all off, or we shan't do justice to the roast beef tonight."

Tim looked at the last slice of toast, decided that he really couldn't manage it, and got to his feet also. They went up to their room and began to get dressed in their full mountain walking kit, winter variety.

Once outside, and ascending the track, the bracing highland air was exhilarating, and the few snowflakes did not bother them at all. They had decided on the northern loop ramble, as they both recognised that they must be responsible about the weather conditions, and this walk would mean that they would not be too far from civilisation throughout the whole of the day. Early on in their Scottish adventures they had had a rather serious conversation in front of the fire in their hotel, after the usual huge dinner, of roast venison on that occasion.

Bill said "Tim, I have been thinking about one thing. Suppose we start taking risks and end up having to call for help. I should feel awful if our stupidity put the lives of those wonderful mountain rescue blokes at risk. I vote we make a resolution never to call them out, whatever pickle we get into. That way we shall learn to be careful and read the mountain terrain and the weather conditions, and plan accordingly."

Tim took a mouthful of delicious whisky, and thought for a minute or two.

"O.K. But you have to remember that the weather up here is not like London. It can change quickly, and be a lot more severe, especially in winter. We must always have our mobile phones just in case. After all, I don't want to be returned to my parents in a body bag, they wouldn't like it at all."

They went on to talk of other things, but they planned their walks with care, and both compass and maps became of great importance.

Now the way was ever upward, and the snow stopped, and even a small patch of blue sky was to be seen. Once a little covey of grouse erupted from the snow covered heather, and flew off with cries of "Go back, go back." It was very lovely on the snow covered mountain, with the higher peaks gleaming in the distance. They plodded on through the morning, keeping an eye on the compass, and once consulting the map, but not saying much. The sky became darker, and looked more threatening. At twelve noon they found a boulder peeping out of the snow, and sat on it to eat their lunch, which had been prepared for them by the hotel kitchen, and stowed safely in their rucksacks. They each had a thermos of tea, which was extremely welcome, as the north easterly wind had picked up a good deal.

The lunch boulder was about the furthest point on their walk, and after lunch they consulted both map and compass and set a course for home base, warmth and good food and drink. How they managed to get the compass bearing wrong they could never afterwards work out, but it meant that they walked south east instead of south west for a couple of hours, as the light began to fade on the short winter's day. Eventually Bill stopped and said

"You know, Tim, we have been this way at least once before, but it really doesn't look the least bit familiar."

"Is that just the effect of the snow, and the fading light?" asked Tim, his voice muffled by the scarf across the lower part of his face. It really was very cold, and the wind chill factor must be huge, he thought. Moreover, it was starting to snow again.

"Just check the compass" muttered Bill. He had not been doing so because it meant taking a glove off, delving deep inside his protective clothing, and getting colder than he already was. Truth to tell, he didn't feel all that well, and wondered suddenly whether the dreaded 'flu was getting him after all.

"That's funny" he said, staring at the compass in his hand. "This thing says we're heading south east." Tim moved closer to him to take a look. Together they squinted at it, then looked out across the snow, in the direction they had been heading. In the fading light, and with heavy snow now falling, everywhere looked suddenly a lot bleaker.

"Suppose we have been walking in the wrong direction" said Tim. "Which way will bring us back to the road to Aviemore?"

Bill struggled to get his thoughts in order. "We must be out to the east," he said at length. "I really don't know how far, several miles at least, perhaps five or six. We must walk west, over that." With his free hand he indicated a steep ridge on their right hand side, which had been growing in height the further they had walked.

Slowly they gathered their things up, and put the compass away. Then shouldering their packs, and gripping walking sticks they set off to scale the ridge. It was not easy walking, to say the least of it, and they floundered into frequent snow drifts as they tried to find some sort of a path. At length, about four in the afternoon, and in complete darkness, they reached the top of the ridge, and were relieved at find a more gentle slope on its western side. But if they had hoped to see the distant lights of welcoming civilisation, they were doomed to disappointment. The falling snow made seeing anything difficult, and they blessed the fact that a small torch was part of their kit, so they could at least keep an eye on the compass. Bill was feeling increasingly unwell, and walking became more and more of an effort, as the cold wind seemed to penetrate his very bones.

The next three hours were the kind of nightmare one longs to wake up and leave behind. It got increasingly cold, and the snow fell heavily. At length Bill called rather feebly to Tim, and leaning on his stick confessed that he was feeling ill and exhausted. They held a brief conference, during which the idea of calling the mountain rescue team was discussed and rejected.

"We decided we wouldn't do it" muttered Bill, "and we don't have a clue where we are, so we couldn't give them any directions anyway."

Tim said "I'll get the brandy out of my pack." He got the rucksack off his back, and rummaged in it until he found the small bottle. They had joked about "just carrying it for medicinal purposes" or to "revive a St. Bernard Dog if they found one in distress!" Now it was reverently passed from Tim to Bill, and after a few sips he did certainly feel a bit better. Bill put the bottle carefully in an inner pocket, and they set off down the slope again. At least going downhill they might find a valley at the end.

They had no idea what the time was when they first saw the light. At first neither commented on it, fearing it might be some sort of mirage. It was away to their right front.

Bill said "Tim, can you see a small light over there?" He stopped and pointed with his stick.

"Yes," whispered Tim through his frozen scarf.

Without further words they changed direction a little and set off again with a renewed sense of purpose. Even so, it seemed that the light hardly grew any nearer, and by the time they reached a stone wall forty minutes later, Bill was in a state of near collapse, and Tim was having to support him. They found a gate, but the snow made it very difficult to open, and Tim left Bill leaning over the wall and tried to shift the newly fallen snow with his boot. At length they staggered up a short garden path, and Tim, having looked in vain for a bell or a knocker, rapped on the door with his stick.

There was silence inside the lighted cottage, and after a half minute had elapsed, Tim knocked again. He was having to physically hold his friend up, as Bills legs seemed to be on the point of collapse.

There was a faint noise inside the cottage, and then a female voice said something, though the sound was carried away by the wind.

"Please help us!" shouted Tim at the door.

"I canna open the door" a woman's voice shouted back. "I'm here all alone."

"Please, please help" shouted Tim. "My friend here won't last much longer."

There was a pause, and then the sound of bolts being pulled back. Slowly the door opened, letting some snow in with it, and by the light Tim could see a small woman standing peering at them. With a great effort he got Bill across the threshold, and the woman helped him get his burden into an old armchair. She then went to shut the door before any more snow blew in.

Tim surveyed the room. It was a typical cottage living room, but better furnished than most, with some pictures and china, and nice wooden furniture, including a small dining table and four chairs. The curtains were thick and colourful, and with a good fire burning in the hearth made the room seem cheerful and warm. Already Bill was looking a little better, and Tim rummaged in his pocket and extracted the brandy bottle.

"I don't think he would have made it without this," he said to the woman, giving Bill a good swig.

"I've got some good broth on the stove" she said, "I was about to be getting my supper but there's plenty for the three of us. By the way, my names Fiona." She had an educated voice, with a lovely Scottish lilt.

"I'm Tim, and this is Bill," said Tim. "I'm truly sorry about this, but we were walking, and got badly lost. Entirely our own fault, and then Bill was not well, - I think he may be getting the 'flu. And then just as we thought we had had it we saw your light."

"I'm sorry I hesitated opening the door" said Fiona. "I'm all alone since my man died in a climbing accident, and we don't get many visitors around here, especially at night. He was a member of the mountain rescue team," she added, "and they got called out on a terrible night, and he was killed. The people that called them out was saved, though," she said, wistfully.

Fifteen Love

She was a slight lass, no more than five foot five in height, and of slim build, with brown wavy hair, and no make up. With blue eyes and a generous mouth she didn't need any, and her jersey and slacks were simple in style and colour. She looked to be about thirty or thirty five, but her face had a hint of sadness that made her seem a bit older. Her beautiful voice struck Tim even more than her attractive appearance.

Fiona went off into the kitchen, and Tim set to work to strip some of Bill's clothes off him, and moved the armchair a little closer to the fire. Fiona came back into the room with a cloth for the table, took a look at Bill, who now looked a lot better, and then put a couple more logs on the fire.

Tim remembered that evening vividly. With food and hot drinks, and small nips of Fiona's whisky, Bill made a very good recovery. Fiona's telephone worked, and Tim was able to call the hotel in Aviemore and tell them what had happened. But when he suggested to Fiona that they try and continue their journey, she went over and pulled back a curtain, looked out and said

"There's no way you two are going anywhere tonight. Look at it now." And she closed the curtain and came back to the fire.

"We can't impose on your kindness anymore" said Tim, smiling up at her.

"I'm afraid I've only the one bed," she said, as if thinking the problem over.

"We shall do fine here" said Tim quickly, "especially if we can make the fire up. I shall keep an eye on Bill, but he can sleep on the sofa with a blanket if you have one, and I shall do fine in the armchair."

"Well, at least you'll be snug and warm, and a lot better than outside. I've plenty to make a good breakfast. I always keep a good stock of food in during the winter, as I never know when I may be cut off. In the morning I'll phone Hector MacPherson, to give you a lift back to the hotel. He's got a good big Land Rover that fair jumps through the snowdrifts!"

After their meal and late night drinks, Tim got Bill settled down on the sofa, and he was soon deeply asleep.

Tim sat in the armchair, in front of the fire, and presently Fiona finished her chores in the kitchen, and came into the room holding a tumbler of whisky.

"Will you have another dram or two?" she asked Tim.

"Yes, thank you very much. But we are drinking all your whisky?"

Fiona chuckled. "Bill won't be drinking any more tonight, that's for sure" she said.

She went over to the dresser, and poured herself out a measure of whisky, and then moved towards the fire.

"Will you come and sit in this armchair?" asked Tim.

"Och, no" she replied. "I'll just make myself comfortable here, if I may" and she settled down on the floor, leaning against the side of the armchair, and touching Tim's leg. He wondered whether to move, but it was so cosy and warm, and the whisky was having a wonderful effect.

"How long ago did your husband have his accident?" he asked in a quiet voice, so as not to wake Bill.

"It's just on four years now," said Fiona, also quietly. "It's been a bad time for me, I get so very lonely. I wanted to go on living in the cottage because David and I did it up together, and he loved it here. But now I'm not sure I'm doing the right thing. One day I shall run out of my savings and the insurance, and I shall have to go somewhere where I can get a job."

They went on talking quietly together, sitting very close to one another. Finally Fiona said "I'm for bed now, before I fall asleep. Thank you for coming, Tim, but I am very worried about you trying to sleep in that old armchair. Although you are not as big as Bill, you'll never be comfortable. I shall worry about you when I'm in my big warm bed upstairs, - although" she added wistfully, "that gets to be pretty chilly on nights like this"

The raw October wind rustled the leaves along the London street, as Bill turned in at the door of the pub, and spotted Tim waiting for him at their favourite table. Tim had already bought a couple of pints for starters.

"Sorry I'm late" said Bill. "Trying to get out of the office on time these days is like trying to leave the clutches of an octopus!"

"Have a good slurp" said Tim, "it's just the right medicine."
They talked of various things, including another trip to the Highlands for about half an hour, and sank another pint.

Presently Bill put on a rather solemn face, and said
"I've got something I need to ask you about, Tim."

"Carry on, old man" responded Tim, tackling his beer with much enjoyment.

"You remember last January in the Highlands, when we got lost?"

"Er Yes" said Tim, with a hint of hesitation.

"Do you remember our kind hostess, Fiona?" asked Bill. Tim looked uncomfortable.

"Yes, of course, Bill" he replied. "Where is this leading?"

Bill looked a little bit like Counsel for the Prosecution down the Old Bailey.

"Tim, when I dropped off to sleep that night, did you go on getting to know Fiona?"

"Well, yes."

"I woke once in the night, Tim, and you were not in the chair. Or anywhere else that I could see. Did you in fact keep Fiona company?"

"Yes" whispered Tim.

"And did you, did you and she, well you know what I mean."

"Yes" whispered Tim.

Bill reached into his inner pocket, and pulled out an official looking letter.

"Tim" he said solemnly, "this morning I received this letter from a solicitor in Inverness. It is about Fiona."

"Oh God" said Tim.

"Yes, precisely" went on Bill. "Now I have to ask you two more things, Tim. When we left, and I was putting on my boots, you were talking to Fiona in the kitchen. Did she ask you for your name and address?"

"Yes" whispered Tim.

Bill paused, and took a thoughtful drink from his glass. Tim looked at him as if hypnotised.

"Tim, did you in fact give her my name and address?"

There was an awful silence. Then Tim spoke, again in a whisper.

"I can't begin to think why I did it, Bill. It was just on the spur of the moment. I didn't think it mattered, really. I never thought she would get in touch, honest I didn't. I know I'm not worthy to claim to be a friend of yours any longer. I just wish to God I could put the clock back." Tim put his arms on the table, and buried his face in them.

Bill waited a few moments, and then took another mouthful of beer.

"Tim" he said, "I have very sad news for you, in fact for both of us." Tim looked up, and there were the marks of tears on his cheeks.

"This letter from the solicitor concerning Fiona" went on Bill, "is to tell me that she was tragically killed in a car crash a few weeks ago. In her will she has left me her cottage and all her savings!"

FIFTEEN. "BUMPSTEAD DREADNOUGHT"

The Bumpstead Dreadnought Char-a-Banc was the creation of the then Rector of Salstead, who in the year 1923 wished to promote the annual choir outing of the Salstead Parish Church Ladies Choir. The Reverend Edgar Loombucket was the first Parson to form a ladies choir in the country, declaring that he loved to see his little ladies showing off their habits, even if the sound they made reminded him of a flock of crows!

The notable char-a-banc began life as a Ford Model A lorry, whose driver lost his head while passing through a low arch into Hedingham Castle in a fit of Medieval bravado. This misplaced optimism also removed the whole of the lorry upper body, but left the chassis and engine mostly intact, and this was a ready godsend for the Reverend Loombucket's inspired idea.

The rector built a platform floor on the lorry chassis, using the base of a disused hen house found in a corner of the rectory garden, and held in place by rather ancient ropes. He then scoured his parish for unwanted items of furniture, and was able to fix about 12 chairs of differing design, together with two sofas and a settee to the floor, using wire, nails and string for fixing.

A problem was encountered when it was noticed that there was no seat for a driver of the vehicle, but the enterprising rector solved the difficulty by providing a long cast off horses saddle, found in a hedge, and fixing it on top of the engine, which was a 4 cylinder petrol-and-steam engine rated at 8 Notional Horse Power or thereabouts. This clever solution proved to have a small flaw when the driver's trousers caught fire ten minutes into the first test run, due to close contact with the exhaust pipe. An offer to provide him with asbestos trousers was turned down with scorn, and new seating arrangements had to be devised which reduced the carrying capacity of the Dreadnought by one. However, the rector condescended to allow one of the choir members to sit on his lap for the journey, which produced a happy solution that gave much pleasure.

The traditional destination of the annual outing was the Village pub at either Steeple or Hellions Bumpstead, - whichever quoted the lower price, where the happy trippers would be entertained with a tripe tea and crackers. This meant a round trip of some 25 miles, by a country route. Sadly, the Bumpstead char-a-banc never managed to reach the tripe paradise. Furniture kept falling off on route, together with passengers, and collisions with a railway bridge, a farm cart, two cows and a load of manure also proved fatal to the enterprise. In addition the engine proved very unreliable, and the head gasket being the source of the steam emissions did not help. Year after year the faithful vehicle was towed back whence it came by a team of smirking horses. One year the rector fixed a poster "Bumpstead or Bust" to the side of his wondrous creation, in a fit of enthusiasm, but it made no difference. They just bust somewhat sooner.

In the years before the Second World War there were many rumours of German subterfuge and dastardly intentions, including the fear that they would invade Salstead by sailing their navy up the river Colne. It was then that the patriotic Rev. Loombucket mounted a small saluting cannon on the bonnet of his char-a-banc, and re-naming it the "Bumpstead Dreadnought" offered its services to the Royal Navy. The Navy were somewhat baffled by the offer, but unwilling to turn down any help, and sent the good Rector a Blue Ensign and copy of the Signal Flags manual, and bade him keep up the good work.

Alas, thus were the seeds of its destruction unwittingly sown. The conscientious Rector, in part hoping for promotion to the rank of Captain Loombucket, which he felt had a nice ring to it, took to patrolling the streets bordering the river at night, looking for U-Boats. He had forgotten, in the eventful summer of 1940, that the mayor of Salstead had a penchant for nocturnal nude bathing. Driving along the lower High Street towards the river bridge, the sharp eyed Rector, fortified with several tots of good old Navy Rum, espied a large bulk rising to the surface of the Millpond. He swung the Dreadnought across the road, lined up on the surfacing U-Boat, and tugged the lanyard of his cannon. The resulting explosion not only delivered a good charge of buckshot into the mayor's hindquarters, but completely obscured the Rectors view with an acrid cloud of powder smoke, so that in two seconds he ploughed through the railings and joined the mayor in his watery but disturbed idyll.

Sadly, the Bumstead Dreadnought was past salvage, even by the team of naval experts summoned from Harwich by the distraught Rector. However, as the ladies choir had all joined up to be Land Girls its services were no longer needed anyway. The poor bereaved Rector was not even permitted the satisfaction of seeing his notable action mentioned in Naval dispatches. He moved on to be a Prebendary of the Cathedral shortly afterwards, and only an inspiring painting by a native of Salstead records those glorious days that are now long past.